"Oh, you're right. It would be easier to just put him to sleep."

George nodded toward Giles without turning his gaze from Willow. The librarian moaned and fell gently to the floor.

"Willow." George smiled gently. "I cannot think of a more appropriate name for what must be done."

Willow looked around. The Druid had her backed against a shelf of books. "Uh, I think I really should be staying here—"

"I'm sorry. That is no longer under your control." He frowned for an instant as his index finger touched his brow. "Willow—Rosenberg, that is correct? You are about to do a very important thing. You are about to save the world."

Oh, Willow thought. *That doesn't sound so bad.*

"I promise you there will be no pain."

Where is Buffy when you need her?

Buffy the Vampire Slayer™

Child of the Hunt
Return to Chaos

The Watcher's Guide: The Official Companion to the Hit Show

Available from POCKET BOOKS

Buffy the Vampire Slayer young-adult books

Buffy the Vampire Slayer (movie tie-in)
The Harvest
Halloween Rain
Coyote Moon
Night of the Living Rerun
The Angel Chronicles, Vol. 1
Blooded

Available from ARCHWAY Paperbacks

BUFFY THE VAMPIRE SLAYER™

RETURN *to* CHAOS

CRAIG SHAW GARDNER

POCKET BOOKS
New York London Toronto Sydney Tokyo Singapore

An *Original* Publication of POCKET BOOKS

POCKET BOOKS, a division of Simon & Schuster Inc.
1230 Avenue of the Americas, New York, NY 10020

ISBN: 0-671-02136-2

First Pocket Books printing December 1998

10 9 8 7 6 5 4 3 2 1

Printed in the U.S.A.

This one's for Barbara and Connie
(the secret Goth girls)

Prologue

EVERYTHING WOULD BE BLOOD AND FIRE.

They were all so simple, so easy to manipulate. The humans were so young, so inexperienced. What kind of knowledge could you gain if you were only given a lifespan of eighty years?

The common vampires were little better. When the first signs of his plan became evident, most of them scattered, leaving the Hellmouth behind, frightened of the power that would come. But moving a few short miles away—moving a continent away—would not save any from his wrath.

The vampires who remained—the foolish, the naive, the inexperienced—these he would use. The humans, no matter their backgrounds or their supposed knowledge, he would use so much more easily.

Already, he could sense the beginning of the

change. His plan, years in the making but an instant in his existence, was gathering force. He could feel the minions of chaos nibbling at the edges of reality. Others less trained than he might sense it soon, but none would be able to discern his true purpose until it was far too late.

And what of the Slayer?

He smiled at that. What irony that the very nature of things would change in the Slayer's own backyard. The Slayer was charged with protecting the world. But when chaos had returned and he was lord of all, the world that the Slayer knew—the world of families and work and high school, the world of human emotions and concerns—would cease to exist.

What would the Slayer protect then?

He decided he would let the Slayer live long enough to see the change; to realize that humans still existed only to serve the whims of the lord of chaos, that he would decide whether they would live or die or go mad. And most of them would certainly go mad. Not that this caused him undue worry. Mad or sane, their blood was still the same.

Only when the Slayer knew the true hopelessness of all that surrounded her—only then would he destroy her. Would he kill her? Would he make her one of his own?

Whatever he decided, it would be a most delicious choice.

Chapter 1

HE SAW IT FIRST IN THE SHADOWS: MOVEMENT IN THE places where the streetlights no longer reached. Quick movement, with hardly any noise. He knew what that meant.

They were being followed by vampires.

Xander Harris sighed. Why did nighttime strolls through Sunnydale always have to come to this?

One of those following them stepped out of the darkness. He just stood there, waiting for their approach. *This,* Xander thought, *is also not a good sign.* But then, vampires and good signs weren't exactly the Doublemint Twins.

"Don't look now," he announced to the young woman walking at his side. "Unidentified Walking Creep at ten o'clock."

Buffy Summers frowned back at her friend. "Ten o'clock. Where's that?"

Xander pointed up at the next corner. "Actually, he's standing under that lamppost." He glanced at his watch. "My mistake. He's standing there at 10:17."

Buffy nodded as she regarded the large, pale fellow who waited farther up the street. "I've noticed a little activity out in the bushes. That's definite vampire material. And check out those clothes."

Xander saw what she meant. The silent, hulking figure wore a dented football helmet, dirty jeans, and a torn, yellow jersey sporting the number thirteen. Xander guessed that was appropriate. Unlucky thirteen. When you were a vampire, Buffy was definitely bad luck.

"Play seventeen," the vampire called.

"What?" Buffy quickly rummaged through the large bag she often carried at night. "What does 'play seventeen' mean?"

"Maybe he just got back from Las Vegas," Xander suggested. Actually, he had no idea what the words meant. So, as usual, he made a joke.

Of course, Xander wasn't exactly the football-player type. After the less-than-wonderful time he'd had on the high school swim team—what with almost being turned into a fish monster and all—he'd sworn off high school athletics for good.

Buffy made a Good!-I've-found-it! sound as she glanced up from her bag. "Too bad he's about six months early for football season."

"Looking at his clothes," Xander replied, "I'd say he was about ten years too late."

"Play seventeen!" the football guy shouted this time. It echoed down the silent street. Xander noticed the shadows moving again.

"Is that all he says?" Buffy remarked as she pulled free one of the sharpened wooden stakes she always kept handy.

"Maybe he stopped one-too-many plays with his head," Xander suggested.

Buffy smiled grimly as she stood, stake in hand.

"I think," she said softly, "that his playing days are just about over."

"Play seventeen!" the big lug announced one more time. He waited, looking to either side. Besides the three of them, the street stayed empty.

"Stood up again, huh?" Buffy called. "I tell you, blind dates can be *really* disappointing."

The vampire looked startled, as if he never expected anyone to talk to him in that sort of tone. Buffy took a step forward, stake in hand.

With your basic bestial roar, the vampire rushed to meet her.

Buffy ran to intercept him halfway, her actions a simple mix of the finest Olympic gymnastics combined with the moves of a Jackie Chan. Every time Xander saw her in action, it still was incredible.

Her rapid approach took the vampire by surprise, too. He made a noise halfway between a shout and a growl, charging forward like he was trying to take out the quarterback. Buffy simply cartwheeled out of the way as the vampire lumbered past.

The big fellow staggered to a halt as Buffy spun

about, ready for his next charge. He turned very quickly for one so large, and rushed to meet her. But Buffy was already into her windup, plunging the wooden stake right into the vampire's heart.

He disintegrated, turning in an instant from a marauding bloodsucker into a bursting pile of dust.

"He had some moves. Too bad they were all wrong." Xander breathed a sigh of relief. No matter how many times he and Buffy ran into this sort of trouble, he'd never get used to it. *Well,* he reassured himself, *they* are *vampires, after all.* This sort of thing could be even more terrifying than high school.

"Uh, Xander?" Buffy called. It was the Slayer's turn to point. "It looks like he brought more of the team."

Three other hulking figures had gathered under the streetlight. If anything, their football uniforms were more torn and disgusting than that of the recently departed number thirteen.

But Xander had other things to worry about, like a rustling, stomping noise in the bushes behind him. Xander was not big on things moving in the bushes. Or, with all that noise, maybe the things were just plain moving the bushes.

The three vampires under the streetlight ran forward. They didn't make any sound at all. *Actually, it's worse when they don't make any noise.* It looked like Buffy would have her hands and feet full for the next few minutes.

Xander turned around.

He saw seven or eight large shapes coming forward through the undergrowth. Even before they stepped free of the shadows, Xander knew what they were. Old number thirteen had brought the whole team. If not for the different colors and numbers on their jerseys, they might have been exact copies of the bloodsuckers Buffy had already faced.

"Hey, fellas," Xander called. If he couldn't beat them, maybe he could distract them. "A little late for a scrimmage, huh?"

The football team paused and stared at him. Well, the distraction bit was working so far. Well, sort of. The whole group of them had begun to growl.

"Sort of mad you didn't get those endorsement contracts, huh?" Xander offered.

Apparently, that was the wrong thing to say. They lumbered forward with a collective roar. He guessed football-playing vampires were not big on subtlety.

Xander took a few quick steps backward. He depended on Buffy for most of the slaying. And Buffy was pretty busy.

Oh, Xander had managed to kill a vampire or two, mostly by accident. He'd also gotten knocked out, roughed up, and almost killed. He expected, facing a half-dozen vampires, that getting killed was the real option here.

The vampires formed a ragged line as they crashed past the bushes. As they came into the light, Xander saw there were a lot more than a half-dozen of them. Like, *really* the whole team. He was not only going to get killed, he was going to be ripped apart. And then they were going to use his head for a football.

"Excuse me, mate!"

Someone—male, young, maybe Xander's age, his head and upper torso hidden by a hood and a flowing cape—had run between Xander and the football line. The newcomer had something in his hands—it looked like a crossbow—and quickly shot a pair of those little arrow things—bolts, yeah, that's what they were called—at the two nearest vamps.

Both vampires staggered back, disintegrating a second later. Whoever the mystery man was, he had great aim.

He also had the rest of the team after him. Xander was forgotten as the vampires rushed the real threat. The mystery guy somersaulted past their first clumsy attack, rolling to a crouch beneath a tree to release another pair of wooden bolts. And he was doing all this in a flowing cape. If Xander ever tried something like that, he would already have tripped and shot himself. *Who is this guy—Batman?*

Two more vampires bit the dust.

"Xander!"

Xander looked over to where Buffy had just impaled the last of her assailants with a dead tree branch.

"Yeah!" he called back to her. "We've got some action over here, too! Somebody new has—"

Buffy had rushed over to join in the attack before Xander could finish his explanation. The mystery guy shot another pair as Buffy kicked a third vampire in the stomach. Xander was feeling pretty useless.

But, hey. The superstars might be on the field, but they needed an equipment guy, didn't they? Xander squatted next to Buffy's bag and fished out another pair of stakes.

"Buffy!" Xander called as his friend went whirling past. He held a sharpened stake in either hand. He felt, more than saw, her pull them away. An instant later, two more of the bloodsuckers were dead.

As, he realized, were all the others. Dead, that is. Mr. Hood-and-cape silently regarded the now quiet and empty street. That was one nice thing about vampires. Since they disintegrated once they were staked, there was no messy cleanup afterward.

Buffy smiled at the newcomer. "Hey, thanks. But we haven't been introduced."

The stranger shook his hooded head.

"I shouldn't be here!"

He turned and, with three quick strides, disappeared into the shadows.

Buffy and Xander were alone.

Buffy sighed. "Oh, well. Just another night in the Hellmouth."

Chapter 2

JOYCE SUMMERS HEARD THE KEY IN THE FRONT DOOR.

"Buffy? Is that you?"

It had to be Buffy, of course. Only Joyce and her daughter had a key. She wasn't really asking if Buffy was home. She was really asking what shape her daughter was in.

It was a part of Buffy's job—that nighttime patrol. But every second or third night, Joyce would look at her daughter and see the danger Buffy was in. It usually wasn't much—a black-and-blue mark on her arm, a cut on her cheek—but Joyce felt every bruise personally.

Buffy healed remarkably fast. She'd look like she had just been in the fight of her life at 11 P.M., then look perfectly fine the following morning. Joyce knew it had something to do with her being the

Chosen One. Or the Slayer. She shivered every time she thought of that last word.

Once they had let Joyce in on their secret, both Buffy and Giles had tried to explain it to her. And she guessed she did understand it somewhat—intellectually at least. Emotionally? That was another matter.

Only one in every generation was chosen, apparently, one who would push back the forces of darkness. It was a great honor, Joyce supposed. *Why does it have to be* my *daughter?*

It was difficult enough moving to a new town, trying to start up a business. Not that her gallery was doing badly. There was something about Sunnydale, some devil-may-care attitude that let people take chances, and that included buying art. But establishing a new business was very time consuming. In their first year or so here, Joyce was afraid she gave far too much time to her business and far too little to her daughter. How else could she not have suspected what was going on? It was only after Buffy had run away from home that Joyce had learned the truth. Now, all she had to do was learn to accept it and find a way to talk to her daughter so she would never feel she needed to run away again.

"Buffy?" she called again.

"Yeah, Mom," her daughter replied in an exhausted voice as she shuffled down the hall toward the kitchen.

Joyce bit her lower lip as Buffy came into view.

Her daughter's pants were torn, and she had a long, ragged scrape running from her left wrist to her elbow. Her blond hair looked like it had been tossed three different ways in a wind tunnel, and her pretty face was marred by a half-dozen smudges, a couple of which looked like blood.

Joyce took a deep breath and tried on her best understanding-mother smile. "Rough night?"

"The worst," her daughter agreed. She gave her mother a quick glance with those piercing blue eyes of hers, as if realizing she might be being too honest. She shrugged. "Not that I was in any real danger or anything."

Joyce really didn't want to know any details. Her imagination was just much too vivid when it came to things happening to her daughter. Still, they needed to keep on talking. And one of the best ways to communicate was to show an interest in your child's pastimes. All the best books said so.

Joyce swallowed. "Vampires?"

Buffy nodded. "The usual, except this time they were wearing football helmets."

"Football helmets." Joyce considered this. "Football playing vampires?"

"We've got all kinds in Sunnydale."

Joyce decided she wanted to change the subject. "Anything else happen tonight?"

"I dunno." Her daughter shrugged again. "I met a guy. Is there anything to eat?"

"There's some leftover chicken in the fridge." Joyce couldn't help but smile. Buffy had met a boy?

That was like a real-world sort of thing; the sort of thing *other* mothers worried about.

"So, tell me about this young man."

For a moment, Buffy was too busy feeding her face to speak.

Joyce did her best not to frown. "You know, you could get a plate."

Buffy swallowed. "Sorry, Mom. I think I ate all of the chicken already. I could go for a glass of milk."

Joyce reached into a cupboard at her side and pulled out a clean glass. Buffy accepted it with a nod and turned back to the refrigerator.

"Now," Joyce tried again. "About this—"

"This guy?" Buffy pulled out the milk carton and quickly filled the glass to the rim. "I don't know much about him. He seems nice. He hunts vampires too."

"Oh," Joyce replied. She didn't know what else to say. She still didn't want to sound upset, but something like "That's nice," simply didn't feel appropriate. It was her own fault, looking for some normalcy in her daughter's life. With Buffy, nothing was ever quite normal.

Buffy sighed as if she hadn't noticed her mother's silence. She finished the glass of milk in three long gulps.

"Not that it matters," she said as she took the glass from her lips. "I doubt that I'll see him again. He's more of a man of mystery."

Like that last boyfriend you had, Joyce thought, *that Angel?* She still wasn't quite sure what had happened there. Trying to talk to her daughter about *that* was absolutely hopeless!

"'Night Mom." Buffy put the glass in the sink and turned to leave the room.

"Goodnight, dear," Joyce said, more by reflex than anything. At least they'd spoken to one another, but it didn't really feel like a serious talk. Joyce realized she really wanted something out of these mother/daughter moments. If her daughter was destined to be the Chosen One, Joyce wanted to be included, too—well, at least in the nice, positive, non-bloody parts of being the Chosen One.

She heard Buffy climb the stairs. It was Joyce's turn to sigh. Perhaps she was rushing things. It hadn't been all that long since Buffy had tried to run away from it all. Maybe things would get better after they calmed down a bit.

Joyce turned on the water to wash out the glass. Things had to calm down, didn't they?

Rupert Giles had once thought this was a good idea. Unfortunately, the printout before him was useless—twenty pages of gibberish, really. They had worked on this for weeks, but for every solution they found, two new problems had taken their place.

He had meant well. He supposed he always meant well.

It had all come about after Buffy's disappearance. Only then had Giles realized how shortsighted he had been. He hadn't a clue about how desperately unhappy Buffy had become. He supposed he hadn't really wanted to see. He could think of no other explanation.

Perhaps I was blinded by my own pain over the loss of Jenny. Giles sighed. A Watcher was not allowed those sort of excuses. He had simply not watched Buffy well enough.

Anyone struggling through their teenage years went through enormous pressures, both physical changes and emotional upheaval. Just because she was the Slayer, why would Buffy be any different? Yet it was a part of his charge that Giles had never considered.

There were other problems in Sunnydale as well. Principal Snyder considered Buffy a troublemaker. Giles had taken care of that. But it wasn't going to be easy for the girl.

The Hellmouth seemed to attract all sorts of supernatural activity. So far, whatever they had confronted, they had triumphed over. But it was all done facing one crisis after another, reacting at the last minute. Some day, Giles feared that something would come along that they couldn't pull together information about in the eleventh hour, something that would destroy them all.

The Slayer, while powerful, was not immortal. Kendra, the Slayer destined to follow in Buffy's footsteps, was now dead. Buffy, and all of them, could easily follow.

Giles couldn't do much to resolve the issues in Buffy's personal life, but maybe he could ease some of the cares of being the Slayer. So he had proposed what he had thought a simple solution to Willow Rosenberg, their resident computer guru and one of Buffy's best friends.

While still only a high school senior, Willow was a genius at looking at that morass known as the World Wide Web and pulling out just the right information. Giles had found her an immense help in his fight with the supernatural. Between Willow's electronic connections and Giles's extensive library of the occult, they could cover almost every situation.

Willow had caught on to what he had wanted right away. "A probability program, right? We get all the icky things that happened in Sunnydale ranked by how likely they are to happen again. Sort of a giant pyramid of ick. That way, we can help Buffy be ready for anything. I can do that."

And perhaps she could, eventually. She had combined her case studies, her research, and all of Giles's historical notes. But rather than an easy solution, all that access caused another problem. There was simply too much information available to them. All of it had potential use, but which of it was really important?

Giles reread the most recent printout—dense pages of words, some in complete sentences, some not. Giles picked a page at random:

"Ten thousand demons await an army of the undead. Uzgrabel, who drinks human tears; Nicoteses, who cracks human skulls; Lianectes, the eater of eyes . . ."

It was all vague and sinister—icky, as Willow

liked to put it. More importantly, Giles couldn't find a context for it to make a great deal of sense.

"Willow—" he began.

She snatched the printout from his hand. "All over the place, right? I can fix that."

Ah, Giles thought, *the optimism of youth.* They would soldier on. And perhaps find a way to tame the Hellmouth for good.

Chapter 3

HE STOOD ON A HILL.

It was the most peaceful and beautiful of hills. The sun was warm, the breezes cool, and the lush grass cushioned his bare feet.

Why was he not wearing shoes?

He looked down and saw that he was naked. For a moment he found this alarming. Not only was he without clothes, but he lacked all of those tools he kept on or near his person, things to protect him both on the physical and mystical planes. Surely, this was a quiet and beautiful day in the least threatening of locations, but why would he venture out without those things he had come to rely on?

He felt a rumbling beneath his feet. The ground, he realized, was not warmed by the sun above them. Rather, it was heated by something below. The grass between his toes became sharp and brittle. The hill below him shook with such force that he nearly lost his footing. He saw a crack open before him in the earth, a fissure from which poured a light so bright it might overwhelm the sun.

This was no peaceful hill. This was no day without care. This was the Last Day—that time when the order that his kind had brought to the world thousands of years ago would unravel at last.

He stood upon that spot where the ending would begin. He recognized the fissures snaking about his feet, knew the horrible light.

For he stood upon the mouth of Hell itself. . . .

He awoke then, his bedclothes bathed in sweat. But his waking gave him no release. He knew the exact meaning of the recent dream.

Quite likely, it was mankind's future.

There is nothing, Buffy thought, *that can't be cured by a good night at the Bronze.* Well, if not cured, at least forgotten for a few hours of good music and good company.

This particular club was the best thing about Sunnydale. Well, the town *was* in sunny southern California with its fabulous weather, but after a while, even fabulous weather could get pretty boring. As for everything but the weather—please! One even had to go to the next town to find a decent mall! But the Bronze, an "all-ages" club that would let you in when you were old enough to have a high school ID; a huge, dark warehouse of a place with live bands three or four nights a week—the Bronze was the perfect place to unwind after a hectic day of the supernatural torment that was high school—a place to get out there and socialize. Or at least what passed for socializing in Sunnydale.

The band was jamming, but she could still hear her friends' voices from twenty feet away.

"Xander!" Cordelia Chase shouted over the music as she marched toward Buffy's table, not to mention purposefully away from Xander. "After what you said back there, I don't even know if we're talking!"

Xander jogged after the statuesque brunette, like a court jester following his queen. Cordelia was dressed tonight in a skintight red number that was halfway between a dress and a pantsuit. But did it really matter what Cordelia was wearing? She looked good in everything. When Cordelia wasn't busy talking, she was into making fashion statements.

"Of course we're talking," Xander called after his retreating girlfriend. "Look. Your mouth opens, your lips move, sounds come out. That's called talking."

Buffy recognized the look on Xander's face—the smart-aleck grin that wanted to say something cutting; lucky for Xander that grin was below those puppy-dog eyes of his that just wanted to be loved. There was part of Xander that never lost that puppy-dog quality.

Xander was dressed in one of his usual choices, a colorful shirt with pants of basic black. The basic scruffy look, the basic I-have-never-even-heard-the-word-fashion look. Buffy was still a little amazed every time she saw the two of them together: the Fashion Queen and Mr. Dressed-Down Teen. If ever there was proof that opposites attract—well, basically, Cordelia and Xander should show up in the textbooks.

Cordelia stopped her march and spun around to fix Xander with one of her patented glares. "You may be talking, but I'm not listening!"

"So, instead of shutting your mouth, you've learned to shut your ears?" Xander taunted.

"I didn't realize we were going to get to see World War Three!" someone shouted next to Buffy, barely making herself heard over the music. Buffy turned to see Willow gesturing across the table at the Xander and Cordy Show. Buffy had been so busy watching the squabble that she hadn't seen Willow sit down next to her.

Buffy nodded. "It's an unadvertised special. 'Come to the Bronze. See hot new bands and a nuclear meltdown'."

Willow smiled in that perpetually perky way she had. Oz plopped himself down next to Willow and grinned, too. Besides being Willow's boyfriend, Oz was perhaps the world's most easygoing human being. Oz was happy. Willow was happy. When the two of them were together, they made Barney the dinosaur look like Oscar the Grouch.

Was Buffy bitter? Nah. Just lonely, and miserable, and looking for the nearest hole where she could hide. But bitter? Well—maybe.

Oz took his turn nodding up at the Xander/Cordelia fight. "And they say nothing happens in Sunnydale."

The band finished playing with a crash of drums. Xander and Cordelia both paused mid-yell. No longer surrounded by rock and roll, they seemed to realize their ever escalating argument might draw a little attention.

Both glanced a little sheepishly at Buffy, Willow, and Oz, suddenly aware of all their friends. "Hey," Xander said. "Everybody knows we have our little differences. Do we need to share them with everybody? I think not." He touched Cordelia's arm. "Maybe we should go someplace private and argue there."

Cordelia looked down at Xander's hand on her arm with an expression that said she had never seen a hand before. Especially that particular hand, which was worthy of a great deal of further study. "Yeah," she agreed. "Private."

Buffy could see the anger drain from both of them as they stared at each other. Xander and Cordelia had been together long enough for Buffy to know every twist and turn of their "opposites attract" routine. They had gone through the opposites part—that was the fight. Now it was time for the attraction. Buffy figured that was the basic rule of the Xander/Cordy relationship: There was no argument that couldn't be solved by a good half hour of necking out by the Bronze's back stairs.

"Cordelia!" a voice shouted from somewhere above. "Just the person I wanted to see!"

Amanda Singer came trooping down the metal staircase from the club's upper level, trailed by three young men. *Interesting,* Buffy thought. Not that—attractive young thing that Amanda was—she wasn't often trailed by various members of the opposite sex, but these particular three appeared to be different. There was *something,* not exactly unfriendly, but guarded, about the way they looked around, like they'd never been in a place like the Bronze before. Her Slayer sense was on red alert.

"Amanda?" Cordelia blinked, released for an instant from Xander's spell.

Cordelia existed in two worlds. One was the cheerleader-centered, popularity-is-everything-and-you're-excluded side of high school; when Buffy had first come to Sunnydale, that was the side where Cordelia had reigned as queen. Now, though, Cordelia had entered the somewhat stranger, definitely geekier side of things that came with Xander and his friends. To Cordelia's credit, she decided to accept both sides of high school, and even put Amanda and her other old buds in their place when they tried to put Xander down.

"Anyway, Cordelia," Amanda's far-too-chipper voice brought Buffy back down to earth. "My three cousins are visiting all the way from England!"

"Wales, actually," said the tallest of the three newcomers. Buffy decided he had a very nice smile. So they were foreigners. They weren't dressed all that foreign. Maybe a little Goth, with black jeans and black sweaters, but nothing that didn't fit into the Bronze. But the foreign thing—that's why she had heard the alarm bells. Giles had told her that she had a special sense, something to do with being the Slayer, that let her know when anything new and different was going on. It was that sense that helped her scope out vampires.

Apparently, it also helped her scope out guys from Wales.

Amanda flipped her long, anything-but-natural-blond hair out of her face. "So, they came over with my uncle, who told me I had to take them out and show them a good time. Can you *imagine?* Well, anyway, I was thinking, who could these three relate to, when I thought of your little friends."

Cordelia frowned. "Amanda. You remember what I said about being cool. Anybody I'm with—"

"—is cool?" Amanda blinked innocently. "Well, of course Cordelia. That goes without saying." She waved vaguely toward Buffy and the others. "Well, I guess I just don't understand them. And I don't understand my cousins, either. No offense, guys. So I figured—well, why don't I just introduce you?"

The tall one in the middle had had enough of this. He stepped forward.

"Hi. My name's Ian. My brothers here are Tom and Dave." Even though he spoke to everyone, Buffy realized he was looking directly at her.

The three of them did look more or less like brothers. All three had pale skin and black hair. Tom and Dave both had somewhat round faces. They seemed younger than Ian, although Dave tried to hide it with a scruffy beard on his chin. Ian's face was more of an oval, with stronger cheekbones than his brothers. That, combined with his soft accent, reminded Buffy of some kind of English lord on *Masterpiece Theater.*

"See?" Amanda chirped. "That wasn't so hard. And these are Xander and Willow and Buffy and—oh, that guy who plays in a band. . . ."

"Oz," the guy who played in the band replied with an all-too-patient grin. Buffy guessed it was all right with Oz if Amanda *never* knew exactly who he was.

"Good. I'm glad *that's* settled." Amanda managed to turn her back on everyone but her old friend. "Now Cordelia. Have you seen Naomi?"

Cordelia frowned. "Not for weeks. Do you have any dirt?"

Amanda fluttered her hands, as if it were all too much. "Well, her father *is* away on a business trip, so maybe it's some kind of *parent* thing!"

Xander sat down at Buffy's table. "Excuse me, but maybe I could talk to some real people?"

Ian frowned. "Cordelia isn't real?"

Buffy smiled up at the three newcomers. "I think what Xander's trying to say is that Cordelia has her own version of reality."

"Gossipland, USA," Willow added.

Both of Ian's brothers laughed at that. Ian frowned at them.

"You'll have to forgive our brother," Dave explained. "He's the eldest, so he's got to be serious enough for all of us."

"It's an awesome responsibility," Tom agreed, "but Ian's up to it."

Ian shook his head and glanced back at his cousin, who appeared to be deep in conversation with Cordelia about Naomi's current hair color. "They are going to go on for awhile, aren't they?"

"Trust us," Xander replied, "we know."

Buffy waved the three newcomers forward. "Sit. Eat."

"Listen," Willow added. "Talk, maybe."

Ian nodded, and the three of them went to search for empty chairs at nearby tables.

Xander looked mournfully at both Buffy and Willow. "Sometimes, I think, there might be some other girl for me."

Willow made a tsking sound. "You don't have the best track record. Mummies, bugs, every woman in Sunnydale wanting you for a love toy? Ring a bell?"

All of them had had plenty of close scrapes with the supernatural—it came with living on top of the Hellmouth. For Buffy, it had been her relationship with Angel, a vampire with a soul. She winced inside. *Will thinking about Angel ever stop hurting?*

And for Xander? Well, the dark and exotic stranger had seemed like a cute South American foreign exchange student, except she really was this ancient mummy whose kiss could suck the life out of a person. And Xander and the mummy had come *this* close to kissing. And then there was that witch's spell that turned horribly wrong. . . .

"Inca Mummy Girls," Xander repeated slowly.

"Every woman in Sunnydale. Oh yeah." He waved at his girlfriend. She continued to ignore him. "Cordelia and I are going to stay together *forever.*"

"Excuse me." Ian and the others were back, chairs in hand. "Did you say something about an Incan mummy?"

Yikes, Buffy thought. It was probably better that strangers didn't hear about that sort of thing. Being the Slayer was supposed to be a secret, after all.

Willow jumped in. "Well, it would be awfully hard to explain—"

"We've heard there are rumors of vampires around here, too," Dave said as he sat next to his brother.

"Rumors?" Buffy asked innocently.

Oz nodded his head. "There's a lot of that going on in Sunnydale—or not."

"Rumors, that is," Willow added helpfully.

Ian smiled. "Exactly. That is why we are here."

Hello! What does this mean? Buffy blinked. There went her Slayer radar again. Ian leaned back in his chair, his face no longer lit by the overhead spots. Seeing his face in shadow like that—that's what she found familiar! Could he be the stranger from the night before?

She leaned across the table toward Ian. "Have we met before?"

Ian smiled. "I haven't had much time to meet anybody."

Well, that doesn't exactly answer my question, does it? An uncomfortable silence settled over the table.

Buffy could hear Cordelia and Naomi comparing the dresses they were wearing to the formal spring dance. Apparently, Badgeley Mischka was favored over Klein. *Again.*

"Well, now you're where the action is," Xander said at last. He glanced sharply at Cordelia. "Whatever action happens in Sunnydale."

"Have you got anything like the Bronze back home?" Willow asked.

"Like the Bronze?" Ian replied. "In Wales?"

Buffy winced. Of course they wouldn't have anything as cool as a California club . . . would they? Well, why should she care if they got embarrassed? Still, Ian was kind of cute, with his dark hair and piercing blue eyes. She decided he wasn't a *Masterpiece Theater* type after all. With his thin nose and high cheekbones, he looked a little bit like a knight of old.

"Like the Bronze?" Tom frowned at that. "I think the local club back home is into a sort of hybrid northern-soul/acid-jazz/jungle thing this week."

"No," Dave added, "actually, that would have been last week."

Tom nodded looking around. "Bands that play their own instruments? It seems very American."

Both of them broke into big grins. Joke city.

"But we didn't come here to discuss the music," Dave continued. "We're here for—"

Ian cleared his throat.

Dave scratched on his excuse for a beard and

looked uncomfortable. "Well, you'd have to ask our uncle."

It was Ian's turn to nod. He was looking straight at Buffy. "If you're who we think you are, he wants to talk to you."

Alarm time. "M-me?" Buffy stuttered. "I'm nobody. Who do you think I am?"

Dave nodded as if he understood all too well. "We no doubt have said too much already."

Ian shrugged. "My uncle doesn't like to talk about anything. Goes with the territory, I suppose."

Uh-oh. Danger, Will Robinson! Her Slayer radar was working overtime. These guys were off the Mystery Meter. Why did they have to be so good looking?

This was the big problem with Sunnydale. Besides worrying about basic stuff like what to wear to the dance and will he ever call you again, every time you met somebody new it could be another Angel or Inca Mummy Girl—or worse.

And speaking of worse—

Amanda bounced up to the table. "So, everybody get to know each other? I hope *so,* because Mom told me I *had* to have you guys home by ten."

Ian smiled at Buffy again. "I think we've seen everything we need to for tonight."

"That's super!" Amanda said, as if she could care less. "And Cordelia and I had a chance to *connect* and compare notes, too. Who knew things would work out so well?"

"Certainly not me," Xander chimed in. "Cordelia, think we might have a few minutes to *talk*, too?"

"Well . . ." Cordelia hesitated. "Maybe . . ."

"But Cordelia!" Amanda whined. "We haven't discussed who we're going to ask to be on the decorating committee."

"What?" Xander asked, incredulous. "Now I'm ranked under the decorating committee?"

Cordelia rewarded him with a pitying smile. "Xander, we have to get the Spring Formal right. It's one of the most important events of our high school life."

"And Cordelia and I are going to make sure it's *perfect!"* Amanda insisted, fluttering her perfectly manicured hand.

"High school life?" Xander asked, more exasperated with every word. "Perfect? What word doesn't fit into this sentence?"

Cordelia glanced at the triumphant Amanda, then back to her boyfriend. "Well, we might not be able to spend all that much time with each other for a while."

Xander looked stricken. "What? What are you trying to say? I know we've been fighting. We always fight! What, do you want a cooling-off period?"

Cordelia glared at him in silence.

"You want a cooling-off week? Month? Year?"

She still gave him the silent stare.

He paused and swallowed. "Do you want to break up?"

Cordelia looked almost as surprised. "Xander,

please! I couldn't possibly break up with you. Not before the Spring Formal."

Cordelia and Amanda exchanged a look. It was obvious that men would never understand.

She leaned forward and gave Xander a quick peck on the cheek.

"I think I'll go home with Amanda and her cousins."

"It's never too early to pick a color scheme," Amanda agreed.

But Xander wouldn't give up that easily. Buffy could almost see the wheels turning in his head; where did these guys get off walking home with his girl?

"Are you sure? What do we really know about these guys?"

"They're Amanda's cousins!" Cordelia replied with a little laugh. "What could go wrong?"

That, Buffy thought, *was the wrong question to ask in Sunnydale.* But when Cordelia had her mind made up, there was no arguing with her.

Cordelia and Amanda were already walking away, chattering in full planning mode. Dave and Tom hurried after them.

Ian paused an instant to smile back at Buffy. "We'll talk again soon. According to my uncle, it's destiny."

So there he goes, Buffy thought. Another good-looking mystery man who liked her. Not that she had such a great track record with mystery men.

Did other Slayers have these problems?

Chapter 4

"WHAT WAS THAT WHOLE THING WITH THOSE GUYS?" Xander said as the rest of them left the Bronze. "Spy vs. Spy? Mission Impossible? The Man from S.U.N.N.Y.D.A.L.E.?"

"It was pretty strange," Willow agreed from where she and Oz followed Xander and Buffy.

"You know," Oz said softly as Willow looked over at him, "we haven't seen each other for three nights."

Uh-oh, Xander thought. Oz was talking about his unfortunate tendency to turn into a werewolf when the moon was full. Three nights every month, like the three that had just passed, he had to lock himself up for safety—his safety, and the rest of Sunnydale's.

"Well, we've seen each other during the day," Willow volunteered.

"Days, yeah. But it's the nights that are important." He looked down to the street in front of him, then back at Willow. "I appreciate you sticking around through all this."

"All what?"

"You know. The hair, the teeth, the claws. The full-moon routine."

Willow hugged him. "No biggie. I think it makes you special."

Xander had had enough of all this true-love stuff, especially after his own night with Cordelia. "Hey, I was talking about the mystery men. Can we stay on topic here?"

Oz nodded sagely. "Their bands don't play their own instruments. Anything is possible."

"Hey, guys!" Willow called. "This is where I've got to split!"

Xander realized they'd reached Willow's house already. He had been so teed off at Cordelia, he had no idea where they were. Life flew by, he guessed, when you're in a snit.

"Yeah," Oz added, "I think I'm going to see her to the door—"

"Yeah," Willow agreed. "To make sure I get inside the house and everything—"

"Yeah," Oz replied. "Well, you know, we could probably talk or something for a minute."

"OK, OK! I get it," Xander said with a sigh. "Buffy and I will keep on walking." He looked over at the blond girl at his side. She'd been awfully quiet ever since they'd left the Bronze.

"Hey," he said gently, "everything OK in there?"

"Huh?" Buffy started as if she had just been woken from a trance. "Oh, yeah." She waved at Willow and Oz. "See you guys. It's been fun."

The tone of her voice still sounded more like deep-down depression than anything resembling fun.

Xander realized that seeing those new guys at the Bronze must have gotten Buffy thinking about her dating life—or lack of same.

Poor Buffy. Ever since she and Angel had had that—falling out, she'd been down on relationships. Then there was that whole business about her skipping town. None of them had gotten over that yet. And now she was walking next to the loneliest guy in Sunnydale. At least, for the moment, her misery had company.

Xander knew of one way to get her mind off relationships. "Is it time for you to go on patrol?"

Buffy did perk up a bit. "I was going to wait until after I walked you home." Buffy generally did a quick tour of the streets just about every night in her role as the Slayer. Vampires and other beasties showed up around Sunnydale with alarming regularity, and it was best to get to them early, before they got any ideas.

"Why don't we walk by the graveyard? See if anything's happening."

"Like maybe we can find another vampire football team?" Xander grinned. "You just want to see that hooded stranger again."

Buffy frowned at him. "I think we just did, back at the Bronze. Actually, I'd like to get that hooded stranger to explain just what he and his brothers are doing here."

"Do you think they're up to something rotten?"

"I didn't say that. But this is the Hellmouth, after all. I'm sure that has something to do with their visit." She glanced at Xander. "I'd say they were here to do something . . . strange."

"I never argue with a Slayer," Xander replied. Besides, walking around those old Sunnydale tombstones would give him something to do. Otherwise, he'd just go home, where his phone was waiting for him—that phone on which he would no doubt call Cordelia.

Now though, he'd be out much later, possibly even facing real danger.

That way, maybe Cordelia would call him first.

Sometimes, Sunnydale could be the most silent place on Earth. And, in moments like this, all her thoughts came crashing in on her.

Buffy didn't know where she was going anymore.

Oh, she knew she was in Sunnydale, headed for the cemetery with Xander by her side. And she knew when she was patrolling she was moving, reacting, doing *something*. It felt so much better than going home.

Buffy hadn't realized how good things were until they were almost gone. When she had sent Angel through the door to Hell, part of her heart had gone with him. After that, she could think of nothing but escaping, of leaving everything else behind. But it was only when she came back to Sunnydale that she realized she had almost lost the rest of her heart as well. By rushing away the way she had, without telling the rest of the gang, Giles, or her mother, she had let them all down.

Buffy sighed. It was only by going away that she realized how much the others needed her. And how much she needed them. Her mother still looked at Buffy like she couldn't trust her. Giles seemed even stiffer than he had before, as if he was at a total loss to understand her. And the others? Sure, the gang all kidded around, but there were moments, silences, when they all felt a little awkward. Before, they all fit together like some familiar old jigsaw puzzle. Now, as much as they tried, Buffy still felt there were some pieces missing.

Angel had come back, but it would never be the same again. They couldn't resume their physical relationship—that was a gimme. And the rest of the gang was still recovering from the emotional wounds his vampiric side, Angelus, had inflicted on them.

Buffy and Xander stopped on the edge of the cemetery. It looked like there was nothing doing here, either.

"Quiet," Xander said at her side.

Buffy almost jumped at the sound of his voice. It wasn't just her mood. There was something in the air tonight, something—quiet or not, that just felt *wrong*. "Quiet should feel better than this."

They nodded and walked forward. The gravestones looked especially pale in the near-full moon. The slightest of breezes rustled the leaves above them and then was gone. There was nothing else.

Quiet.

They walked back out through the cemetery gate.

"Well, exercise is good for all of us," Xander said.

"Builds strong bodies twelve ways," Buffy agreed,

"There's no avoiding it. I guess I'd better go home and make *that* call."

"And I'll go home and see Mom."

Xander looked at her for a moment. "This doesn't sound like a happy thing."

"With my Mom? It's Big-Frown Time." Ever since Buffy had gotten back, her mother had become even more overprotective, as if knowing about Buffy's special powers was nothing more than an extra reason to worry.

"Parents," Xander agreed. "Can't live with 'em, can't live without 'em."

"At least not 'til you're eighteen," Buffy added.

"So let's get out of this fun spot." He glanced back at the rows of graves. "The Vampire's Plunge O' Death. A real E-ticket."

"Hey! There can be worse rides."

Xander nodded. "At least here there are never any lines."

They headed home.

Sometimes, Cordelia just needed her space.

Xander certainly could be impossible. If only he

didn't kiss like—no, Cordelia didn't want to go there right now. Sometimes it was best not to examine things too closely. The two of them were just another of the unexplained mysteries of Sunnydale.

What exactly was she doing with Xander, and why did she miss him so much when he wasn't around?

She wished she could share some of this with Amanda. Not that they could talk all that freely in front of Amanda's cousins.

Still, life could be worse than taking a nighttime stroll with three cute guys. *Maybe I can draw them out, even do a little serious flirting. . . .*

She sidled up next to Tom. He had the broadest shoulders of the three; he looked like he worked out. "So, what do you guys like to do? Sports?" No reply. "Cars?" Still nothing. "Spend money on girls?"

Tom didn't even look at her. He was too busy studying the streets in front of them. She *had* seen both Tom and his brother Dave laughing back at the Bronze. Now they seemed to be all business.

"We don't have any time for sports."

Oh. What else could she talk about? Well, they *were* from Wales. "Do you travel much?"

Tom shook his head. "First time away from home."

His brother Dave frowned at Cordelia. "We've talked too much." He looked to Ian. "What were you thinking?"

"We shouldn't talk about it," Ian replied grimly.

"If our uncle ever found out—" Dave began.

"We can't talk about that," Ian replied.

That, apparently, was the end of the conversation.

Was this whole conversation supposed to creep her out? If it was, they were doing a good job. It sounded like she was walking right into the middle of some sinister plot. Still, these guys didn't look particularly dangerous. And Amanda was maybe the least sinister person Cordelia knew.

Maybe they were behind some new nefarious plot. But knowing what went on around this town, it was just as likely some evil witch or a giant lizard from beneath the earth was behind the plot instead.

Why am I thinking this? Is this supposed to be reassuring?

She was starting to miss Xander already.

What was she thinking? Leaving Xander at the Bronze, coming home like this, she didn't even get a good-night kiss.

Compared to them, Xander was Mister Charming. Well, Xander was charming in sort of a geeky way. And the way he kissed!

No, Cordelia, reminded herself. *Not going there. . . .*

She hardly remembered what they were fighting about. It had seemed so important to talk to Amanda about the big dance, but they had hardly talked at all since leaving the Bronze. The formal didn't seem all that important if Xander wasn't a part of it. She could see the dance now. She would be stunning in a lavender gown. Xander could just tag along and make his usual dumb comments. It would be a perfect evening.

Cordelia sighed. At least her entourage had walked her home in one piece.

"Hey, this is my place," she called to the others. "It's been real."

"Thanks for keeping me company with the three wise men here." Amanda looked at her watch. *"Eep!* We're half an hour late! My uncle is going to *kill* us! See you, Cordelia."

Amanda and her cousins trotted quickly down the street.

Cordelia walked up the front steps. *Where is my front-door key?* Cordelia frowned. *Why do I carry all this stuff?* Even in her smallest purse, it could take her five minutes to find her keys.

She heard something, out on the front lawn. A scraping sound, she thought, and maybe a voice.

The sound was very faint. Yes, it was definitely a voice.

"Cordelia."

Someone had called her name, but the sound hadn't been much more than a whisper.

"Cor - de - lia . . ."

Louder this time, her name sounded almost musical, the syllables rising and falling in tone.

A young woman stepped out from behind the bushes—a young woman dressed in flowing white. It was someone Cordelia hadn't seen in quite some time.

"Naomi!" she called. "We were just talking about you. You know, me and Amanda. She's just down the street. I could call her back in a second."

But Amanda and the others were already out of sight. Where were those three dull guys when she needed them?

"Sweet Cordelia," Naomi said. She seemed to be able to talk without moving her lips.

Something was definitely different about her. Maybe it was that new hair color Amanda had been talking about.

She was coming closer. She was so light on her feet, she almost seemed to glide across the front lawn.

"Gee, Naomi. You look awfully pale. Have you been getting enough sun?"

Naomi smiled.

Chapter 5

HE WAS RUNNING FROM THE HELLMOUTH. BUT THE fissures grew ever larger around him, spitting great gouts of fire. He would fall into a crevice or be burned alive.

"Where are you going, brother?"

Before him, floating in the air above the flames, was his brother Stephen.

"What do you hope to do?" Stephen continued.

"I—have—to—get—away." He was having trouble forming words.

"There's no way you can flee," Stephen said gently. "The only way to escape is to confront the Hellmouth."

"Confront these things? I saw what happened."

"We were not ready before. We were led down false paths. You must find the truth."

"The truth?" he demanded. "What is the truth?"

But his brother had let himself drift too close to the flames. Fire engulfed his form. He staggered back, waiting for the screams.

But Stephen laughed instead—a hideous laughter that filled the air around him—a laughter that would consume him as surely as fire.

"This program! Why can't anything go easily around here?"

Buffy heard Rupert Giles before she saw him. She pushed open the swinging doors that led into the Sunnydale High School library.

To the rest of Sunnydale High, Giles was the school librarian. A tall, thin fellow with horn-rimmed glasses, Giles had a distinct British accent and was probably as old as Buffy's mother. But he was also Buffy's Watcher.

What exactly did a Watcher do? Even now, Buffy wasn't exactly sure. Giles wasn't even her first Watcher. She'd had another fellow who helped her out, Merrick, over at her old high school, Hemery High in Los Angeles. That was, of course, before she burned it down and had to move to Sunnydale. Buffy had been able to defeat the vampires at her old school, but not before they'd killed her Watcher.

Buffy was determined never to have anything like that happen again.

And what exactly was a Watcher? Well, as far as she could figure out, Giles was part mentor, part trainer, and part walking encyclopedia of arcane knowledge and spooky stuff. Throughout history, there had always been Slayers—born into every generation—to push back the forces of evil. As far as Buffy knew, they had all been young women close to her age. And all those Slayers had always had Watchers to guide them on their way.

Generally, they watched out for you. Buffy thought that having a Watcher was one of the nice things about being the Slayer. Giles had helped her a hundred times, and when she had enlisted some of the other kids at school to help, he had accepted her friends as well. Buffy thought he was sort of like a scout leader of the occult.

Right now, though, this particular scout leader was not a particularly happy camper.

"Hey!" Willow called. "At least it's printing out complete sentences now. Too many complete sentences." She glanced back at the monitor. "Way too many."

Giles paced back and forth behind the library table where Willow scowled at the computer. Buffy was the third person to enter the large, book-filled room. It was still pretty early in the morning, with maybe half an hour before classes, but the other students at Sunnydale High didn't seem to have that much use for the library. Which was too bad, really. The high-ceilinged room was maybe half the size of the school auditorium, with long tables perfect for reading or studying. A few of the tables even had computers, just like the one Willow was using.

Beyond Willow, steps led up to even more books—it was sort of a split-level library. It was up there, at the back of the room, that the more common books on the occult were kept. Thanks to Giles, the library had quite a few. He even had a small, locked cage behind the librarian's desk where he kept the really rare, one-of-a-kind stuff.

Buffy often wondered what the other students and teachers thought of Giles's somewhat lopsided collection, not to mention the locked stacks. The one time she had mentioned the subject, Giles had sniffed rather self-importantly and said the administration here should feel privileged to be able to employ a librarian of his stature. That he should bring a few of his own research materials along went without saying.

But if Giles was the scout master, then this room was also summer camp all year round for Buffy and her friends. Giles never minded any of them dropping by, even on those days when there wasn't a crisis. This library really felt like Buffy's home away from home.

Of course, some days at home were better than others. Apparently, the librarian's research wasn't going all that well at the moment.

"Is there *any* way we can fix this?" Giles moaned,

Willow glanced up at Buffy and grinned. "Hey, with computers you can do just about anything." Willow's faith in computers was one of the constants of Sunnydale. "And here we have just about everything."

"Everything," Giles added in his usual distracted manner, "and more than everything." He waved at the stack of printouts piled next to the library's laser printer. They were the size of two large phone books. "This is what's going to happen to Sunnydale!"

This was all going too fast for Buffy. "Wait a moment! This is the big computer project you started last week, right? The one that was going to make our lives so simple?"

Giles peered at her over his glasses. "Well, it did appear it would be simple at the time. The—what did Willow call it?"

"The 'Let's Give Buffy a Break' program," Willow added helpfully.

"Yes, it was supposed to make life easier—sort of an early-warning system for potential disaster areas." He shook his head. "I was quite exact in what I had Willow load into the program. All the experiences you've had since you've come to Sunnydale—"

"All my experiences?" Buffy demanded.

"Only those that have to do with you being a Slayer," Willow reassured her. "I've been keeping a file."

"And we also compiled files on the history of Sunnydale and its surroundings," Giles continued, "concentrating on unexplained occurrences in the past."

Buffy could see what they were getting at. "You mean sort of a life story of the Hellmouth."

Giles paused, the slightest look of surprise on his face. "Well put. Then, not knowing what else would be pertinent, we also added all the research we've done on earlier events, whether or not that research was useful at the time. And, after that, Willow and I added whatever pet projects we'd been researching—you know, about the occult, the supernatural, special phenomena, the 'funky' as you call it."

"Wow," Buffy replied. "Did you also throw in the kitchen sink?"

"I wish we had. That, at least, we'd know how to turn off."

"So, what you're telling me is, this whole big project hasn't worked."

"No, not at all. The problem is that it worked too well." He patted the very large stack of printouts. "This was supposed to be an early-warning system for you, so we could nip some of these dangers in the bud, so to speak, and not have a new crisis every week. Alas, this program has revealed the true, overwhelming nature of our task."

Willow looked up from her work at the computer. "Like Giles said, the problem here is that it's all too easy. Since Sunnydale is located right over the Hellmouth, everything is likely to happen."

"Everything?" Buffy was beginning to see what had Giles so flustered. This was beginning to upset her, too.

"Well, not *everything.*" Willow hit a few buttons on her keyboard. New text filled the screen. "It's unlikely we'll have an earthquake in the next couple months." She paused then added, "Rainfall looks a little down for the season. And—um—we're not due for a plague of locusts until at least July." She looked up at Buffy with that what-ya-gonna-do look of hers. "But beyond that, we're up for grabs."

But Buffy refused to accept defeat—probably something to do with being the Slayer. Maybe both Willow and Giles were too close to the problem. "Look guys. How big can this be?"

Giles shook his head. "Maybe we can show you the true nature of our problem. Willow, why don't you choose one of the smaller subcategories of danger that our program generated. Something, say, with less than twenty items?"

"Less than twenty?" The tone of Willow's voice said that was going to be tough. She once again scrolled through the text on her screen. "Well—maybe 'Monsters from the Sea.'"

"Monsters from the *sea?"* Buffy replied.

"Hey, Sunnydale has a beach, doesn't it? Some pretty cool scenarios here." Willow frowned at the screen. "Here's one where we're overrun by sentient seaweed. Oh, and killer clams." She grinned. "I particularly like the one with the mutant whale with feet."

"Feet?" was Buffy's only response.

This time, Giles's sigh seemed to go on forever. "You can see the sort of thing we're up against.

Buffy was afraid she did. "Instead of limiting the possibilities—"

"The computer program seems to go to great lengths to make up *new* ones," Giles continued.

"Now, some of these possibilities sound pretty unlikely—"

"Around Sunnydale?" It was Buffy's turn to shake her head. "Anything is possible."

Giles waved at the stack of paper behind him. "I didn't say these were in any way inaccurate. However, we weren't simply looking for the possible. We were looking for the probable. That was the original purpose of the program, to predict what we needed to prepare for. We needed to know what was likely to happen next week. Unfortunately, that word—likely—seems to have been left out of the final mix."

"So we don't have to prepare for mutant whales with feet?" Buffy asked.

"Heavens. I hope not."

Well, Buffy thought, *that was good news at least.* Maybe there was a way out of this mess. "Is there some way to rescue all this? How many possibilities are we talking about?"

Giles paused for a long moment before he answered. "That's very difficult to say. That category of dangers that we just read—"

"'Monsters from the Sea,'" Willow added helpfully. "And we only read a little bit of it. I didn't even get to the vampire sharks—"

"Yes, 'Monsters from the Sea'," Giles quickly interrupted, "is only one of many."

"How many?" Buffy asked.

Giles grimaced. "Seventy-three."

Wow, Buffy thought. *"Only* seventy-three?"

Giles's grimace didn't go away. "So far. When we saw what was happening, we stopped the program."

Willow nodded solemnly. "I think it could have generated dangerous scenarios . . . forever."

"No doubt we've learned something from all of this." Giles smiled weakly. "There might be very valuable information in here—*somewhere.*"

Buffy pointed to the printouts. "So, could we deal with the stuff we have so far?"

"Hmm." Giles stuck his tongue in his cheek as he considered the possibilities. "Based on our response time in the past? I'd say, with the advanced technology at our disposal, and all of us—we three, along with Xander, Cordelia, and Oz—all working together, in all our free time, we could sort through it all in—maybe three years."

"Three years?"

Giles smiled. "Rest assured, Buffy. None of us want to spend another three years in this particular high school."

Buffy was beginning to see the true depth of their problem. "By college, I was hoping to have some better things to do. I was hoping Slaying might lead to a career."

"Well, this is not really worth thinking about. All the current program can do is upset us. It all seems overwhelming."

But Willow was wearing her bravest smile. "We'll find a way to get this darned program to work." She looked down to the computer in front of her. "Well, I'll find a way."

Giles nodded. "We've beaten every challenge that has been put before us." He began to pace again behind the table. "There's no reason not to believe that with a little luck and preparation we might be able to defeat whatever else we encounter. Even a computer program."

Willow frowned down at her monitor. "It seemed to make so much sense when we began." She started to type.

This is where I came in, Buffy thought.

"There's got to be some way we can limit our parameters," Giles muttered, more to himself than anyone else. "These results are less than useless. . . ."

"Gotta go!" Buffy called. She was sure she had a couple other things she had to do before classes started.

Still, she had rarely seen the pair looking so glum. There had to be something upbeat Buffy could say.

"Hey," she called over her shoulder as she pushed open the library door, "when you're prepared for a mutant whale with feet, you're prepared for anything."

They didn't even bother looking up at her as she left the library.

Chapter 6

WHY COULDN'T CORDELIA REMEMBER?

She had been standing at her front door, searching for her keys. Absolutely nothing strange in that. Then someone had—what? She had almost more felt than heard somebody call her name.

It had to be Amanda or her cousins, right? Why did this make her so upset? She couldn't think of anyone less spooky than Amanda. Well, there was that time Amanda had gone through a phase and dyed her hair that weird shade of red, but that was more mind-blowing than spooky.

All morning, from the moment she'd gotten out of bed all the way through climbing the steps to the high school, she'd had the feeling that something was—missing. She wasn't even sure if that was the right word.

It was more like something was—*wrong*. Something she had to make right again. But how could she make something right if she couldn't even remember what it was?

She had maybe five minutes before homeroom. She stared into her locker, as if the answer might be hidden somewhere between her chemistry text and her lunch.

She got a glimpse of herself in that small mirror she had hung on the back of the locker door. There were circles under her eyes so large that even her concealer couldn't hide them. She looked like she hadn't gotten any sleep at all.

Cordelia blinked. It wasn't her face looking back in the mirror. The face was very pale, as if the person almost wasn't there. She had seen that face—it seemed like only moments ago. A pale girl—she knew her, didn't she? Cordelia couldn't look away. The eyes drew her deeper and deeper. She heard someone call her name, but it was not really a sound. It was more like a breeze, crawling up her spine—

"Cordelia?"

She jumped about a foot when the hand touched her shoulder. She spun around in a second, ready to fight or run.

It was Xander.

She half-wanted to hug him, half-wanted to bop him for sneaking up on her that way.

She decided she'd yell at him instead. "Don't scare me like that!"

Xander took a step away, like scaring her was the

last thing on his mind. "Sorry. I thought maybe we could take a minute to talk about—uh—last night."

"Last night," she repeated. What really had happened last night? She and Xander had fought about some silly thing or other. It didn't seem at all important now. Then she had talked with Amanda forever. They had walked home together. And there had been Amanda's dreary, but cute, cousins.

Why can't I remember what happened next?

"Look," Xander persisted, "about last night . . ."

As upset as Cordelia was, she realized she wanted to patch things up with Xander. The two of them could get so intense around each other, for good or bad. Sometimes Cordelia thought that intensity was the only thing holding them together.

"Do you mean at the Bronze?" she asked innocently.

Xander shrugged. "Well, you know, sometimes I get—"

She wasn't going to let him take all the blame. She wanted this relationship to work.

"Look," she interrupted, "that's nothing compared to the way I—"

Xander interrupted her right back. "Well, look, when I said—"

"Xander," she interrupted all over again. "I never really gave you a chance to—"

There was the bell. What bad timing!

Xander smiled at her and squeezed her shoulder. "Well, I'm glad we at least had a chance to talk."

She waved to him as he turned to go. "Later?"

"Later!" He gave her a glimpse of his incredibly cute grin.

Why was his touch so electric? And why did they have to go through an entire day of high school before they could—well, actually Cordelia had all sorts of creative ideas involving the janitor's closet. Creative ideas that had nothing to do with the Spring Formal. Not that Xander wouldn't look very nice in a tux. For all of the little problems the two of them had, it was awfully nice to have a steady boyfriend around for the important events.

Why was she so worried? Xander and she had just made up. She was on the committee controlling the big dance. She had even gotten an A on her chemistry midterm.

Cordelia frowned. Well, that was all well and good, but there was one other thing she couldn't forget:

"I must satisfy my mistress."

Cordelia stopped breathing. She realized she had said that aloud. She barely recognized her own voice. Thank goodness it was almost time for school to begin, and everybody was too busy rushing to their homerooms to listen to what was coming out of her mouth.

Where did that *come from, anyway?* "I must satisfy my mistress?" It sounded like the sort of thing that happened to Buffy Summers, not Cordelia Chase. Maybe she should ask Buffy. Or Giles. He seemed to know almost everything.

Wait . . . Cordelia swallowed as a new thought

blossomed deep in her brain. Maybe this was happening because she was too involved with them already. *Maybe I've been hanging around Buffy too much.* Maybe she had to get away from that whole crowd—then she'd be just fine. Well, not the whole crowd. She and Xander could think of other things to talk about.

Cordelia shook her head. She and Buffy had been getting along pretty well lately. Now, though, even thinking of Buffy made her a little uneasy.

This just got stranger and stranger. Oh no. There was the final bell. She'd be late!

Right now, she was glad there was a little time before she'd be seeing Xander again.

With Xander around, Buffy couldn't be far behind. She almost shivered.

Cordelia took a deep breath. Maybe, with a full day of classes, she could clear her head.

At last, Oz thought, *I can get back into the swing of things.*

For the last three nights, the nights of the full moon, he had to lock himself away in the cage at the library. But now that the full moon had passed, he could think about other things. His band was getting regular local gigs the other twenty-five days of the lunar cycle. They'd played at the Bronze now a half-dozen times, and would be playing at Sunnydale High for the Spring Formal. The only problem with that was, since he was in the band, he couldn't really get to spend that much time with Willow, who was a pretty amazing girl. Besides being cute and sexy and smart, which was also sexy, Willow accepted him completely. And she had a bunch of friends who not only knew about his other life, but didn't really seem to care. It was pretty keen to be able to share that kind of secret.

Besides the werewolf bit, Oz guessed life was pretty great.

He'd made it through another whole day of classes. Not, of course, that Oz paid much attention to that sort of thing, but since he was repeating his senior year, Oz did have to keep up some appearances. Now it was time for the all-important socializing.

Willow wasn't in the computer lab or student lounge, so he figured he'd find her in the library. He pushed through the swinging doors. Sure enough, she was staring at a computer screen.

"Hi." He nodded as she looked up at him.

"Hi," she said without much feeling.

Something must be up. She hardly gave him any smile at all. That meant she was really worried.

"So, what's up?" he asked.

That was her cue. She looked back up at him with a big frown. "It's all so impossible."

Oz just nodded. Around Sunnydale, a lot of things were impossible. He guessed being a werewolf gave him a little extra perspective.

"See," Willow explained, "Giles and I had been working on this program all weekend. The prediction program?"

Oz nodded. When he and Willow had finally gotten back together last night, it was all she wanted to talk about. Well, when they were talking.

Willow just frowned back at the computer screen. He figured she was stuck in more ways than one.

"So something went wrong?" he prompted.

"It was too successful. Instead of warning Buffy about dangers, we came up with enough dangers for a hundred Buffys. We got tons and tons of possibilities. Killer clams. Vampire sharks."

"Uh-huh." Oz urged her along.

"Whales with feet," she added.

Oz was patient. He knew she'd get to the point sooner or later.

"But that was this morning. Now, everything's gone away." She looked back at the screen like it was the end of the world.

"You mean, like all those dangers aren't there anymore?"

Willow nodded. "Something's wrong."

"Huh?" Oz had to get this straight. "Something went wrong with your program that was going wrong?"

She smiled gratefully. "I couldn't have expressed it better myself. I knew we were going together for a reason."

Well, Oz guessed he was glad somebody was happy. "Uh, Willow? I'm not exactly sure what I just said."

"Well, like I said, we were just getting too much

data. Some of it might have been useful, but there was no way to tell. So, to try and figure out what was going on, I convinced Giles that we should upload one more day's worth of data, see what kind of new possibilities it generated. But we'd separate the types of data—feed in the local news first, say, then the weather report, then my daily update on Buffy—"

Oz was impressed. "You did all that?"

"And a lot more. We had plenty of variables. Maybe that was our problem. Anyway, if I isolated each piece of data, I could study the effects of each on the whole program."

She was frowning again. Oz ended up smiling at her anyway. He loved it when Willow explained things.

"Makes sense," he agreed.

"But everything went away!"

"Everything?"

"Just about. Right between the news and the weather. All those dangerous scenarios the computer was spitting out the day before—it was like they never existed."

"So now nothing's going to happen in Sunnydale?"

Willow shrugged. "Well, nothing that much out of the ordinary. The program's telling me there's still a couple of possibilities that have to do with vampires."

"Oh, well, what else is new? This is Sunnydale, after all."

"Exactly."

"And these vampire things are the sort of stuff Buffy can handle?"

Willow nodded. "Any day of the week."

"So all your problems with the program went away."

Willow nodded again. "And all the problems *in* the program went away, too."

He thought about it for a moment before adding, "Isn't that a good thing?"

"Well, it could be a good thing," Willow admitted. "It certainly looks like a good thing."

He took a couple of steps closer to Willow. She seemed to be relaxing a bit.

"Well, that's good. I like good things."

She looked him straight in the eyes and smiled. "I like good things, too."

Were they talking about the computer program anymore?

Willow shook her head. The moment was gone. "I just can't stand not knowing. It's not the program. It's something else. I think something changed as a result of the data we fed it this morning."

"And this something—is it good, too?"

Willow shrugged. "Maybe good. Maybe bad. To make all that stuff change, it would certainly have to be powerful."

"How powerful?"

"To stop the possibility of all those horrible disasters? I'd say it would have to be end-of-the-world powerful."

Uh-oh, Oz thought. *Now we're getting down to it.* Being around Buffy, they'd survived a couple of end-of-the-world things already. Survived, but it was nobody's idea of a good time.

"So," he summarized. "Not having any problems could be a real problem."

Willow nodded. "I think I want to talk to Buffy."

Chapter 7

BUFFY COULD SENSE IT IN THE AIR. IT WAS ALMOST spring, and the night was pleasantly cool. The streets were quiet. She hadn't seen a soul in the last fifteen minutes of her patrol. Not a pedestrian, not a delivery van, not even a police car. Everything was perfect.

She knew the vampires were out tonight.

This sense was born in her, a part of her birthright. Even Giles, who had helped her find it in herself, couldn't really explain where it came from. But a Slayer was able to sense danger—especially supernatural danger—before it happened.

After all, Buffy thought, *who else is going to save the world?*

It began like a tingling in the back of her skull, causing her to snap to full alertness. *They're out there,* the feeling said, *preying on the innocent, looking for blood. They want to destroy everything good.*

There were certain nights, like tonight, when that feeling was very strong. *Closer. Closer.* And it was getting stronger with every passing minute.

The scream came from just around the corner.

Buffy ran toward the noise, sizing up the scene as soon as she saw it. She had run into the parking lot of one of those new condo complexes. The young woman—the one who screamed—was maybe college age. She had just gotten to her car when the vampires attacked. The car door hung open, the keys still in the lock. There were two vamps, one male, one female. They seemed to be playing with their victim, like cats might toy with a mouse, letting her get halfway back to her car before blocking her way, forcing her into a corner, then backing off, giving her the illusion that she might escape.

"Hey, guys," Buffy announced. "Game's over."

Both vampires spun at the sound of Buffy's voice.

"Another one!" said the male half of the vampire tag team. "We'll drink our fill tonight."

"Oh, Bernie!" his female counterpart replied. "You always could show a girl a good time."

Both of them smiled, showing their fangs.

"Get away from here!" the college woman called to Buffy. She was breathing heavily, exhausted by the chase. "They're monsters!"

"Not for long," Buffy replied. She had already pulled a wooden stake from her shoulder bag. Bernie? It didn't seem like a really good name for a vampire. Not that he'd have to worry about it for long.

"They said we'd never make it on our own," Bernie crowed as he advanced on Buffy. "Said we needed a plan."

"Yeah, Bernie," his female counterpart agreed. "Who needs a plan when there's fresh blood everywhere?"

They? Buffy thought. *Who the heck are "they?"*

Not that she'd have a chance to ask. Bernie was already rushing toward her.

"I got dibs on this one!" he called, looking back over his shoulder. "You take our—"

He ran right into Buffy's stake, disintegrating midsentence as she pulled the stake out. She had probably killed hundreds of vampires by now, but this was the first time she didn't even have to move to do it.

His partner got a little upset. "Bernie!" she squealed. "What did you do to Bernie?"

"Don't worry," Buffy replied grimly. "You'll be joining him shortly." She waved the sharpened wood in her hand. "I'll even use the same stake." She strode toward the second bloodsucker.

"Oh, no you won't!" The female vamp took a step away. " 'We don't need any of the others,' Bernie says. 'We go out on our own, we'll get fresher pickings,' Bernie says. 'Why listen to them?' Bernie says. I should have listened!"

Buffy paused in her advance. "Who's 'them?' "

The vampire frowned. "You're that Slayer person, aren't you? 'It's a big town,' Bernie says. 'What are our chances of running into the Slayer?' Bernie says. Our chances were pretty darn good!"

Buffy didn't have much experience dealing with hysterical vampires. Any vampire was dangerous; an emotionally unpredictable one might be even more so. But if this shrieking vamp would keep on talking, she might let on to some bigger plans.

"I don't need to kill you right away," Buffy said soothingly. "Why don't we talk about it?"

"'Why don't we talk about it,' she says?" the female vamp mocked. "'Hey, Gloria,' Bernie says. 'It's you and me against the world,' he says. 'Sort of like *Rebel Without a Cause,'* he says, 'except James Dean is a vampire.'" She shook her head. "I was always a sucker for a nice set of fangs."

Gloria? Buffy thought. She guessed it wasn't any worse than Bernie. Past Gloria she could see the young woman who'd been attacked was leaning heavily against the car.

Buffy waved her stake. "Well, Gloria, why don't we move out of the way and let this nice lady get back in her car."

"No way! We're talking about my dinner, here!"

Buffy took a casual step in Gloria's direction. The vampire's gaze focused on the stake.

"Oh, OK, maybe I'm being a little hasty here. I always let Bernie do all the thinking. It's tough. One minute you're with a guy, the next he's crumbled to dust."

Lost love, huh? Tell me about it. For an instant, Buffy actually felt a little sorry for this vampire. Not that it had anything to do with Buffy's situation. Love, shmuv. She'd had enough of this.

"No hard feelings." She took another step toward Gloria. "You're a vampire, I'm the Slayer; let's get this over with."

Gloria took another couple of steps in reverse. "No way! 'Let's all do this together,' they said. 'They never gave us a chance before. Now's our time.' I should have listened. I'm going to go and listen now!" She turned and jogged quickly away, only pausing when she was a hundred yards down the street. She cupped her hands to her mouth and yelled:

"When I come back, little miss Slayer, I won't be alone!"

The woman by the car moaned and slid to the ground.

Buffy sighed. She could chase after the vampire, but their intended victim was still in pretty bad shape. Buffy turned her attention to the young woman. She looked basically intact—Bernie and Gloria had been too busy playing with her to do any serious biting or bloodsucking. The young woman was breathing heavily, her clothing torn. She had sunk to her knees during Buffy and Gloria's conversation. She stared up at Buffy now like she was in shock.

"Are you all right?" Buffy asked gently.

The woman blinked. "Who are you? Who were they?"

How could Buffy explain? "Think of them as

muggers with really big teeth. Trust me. You don't want to walk around this town by yourself after dark." She offered the woman her hand. "Why don't we get you into your car?"

The woman nodded and allowed Buffy to help her up.

"Do you think you'll be okay to drive?"

"As long as I'm driving away from here," the woman agreed. She grabbed her keys from the car door and slid behind the wheel. "I go to State College. I live in a dorm less than a mile away from here."

Once she was in the car, Buffy thought she would be safe. After what had just happened to her, this woman wasn't about to stop for any strangers. And there were always people around at a college.

The woman looked up at her as she started the car. She opened her window a crack so they could talk.

"You still didn't tell me who you were."

Buffy grinned. "I'm somebody who knows how to handle muggers. Especially this kind."

The woman shook her head. "Maybe I should be taking those self-defense classes after all. I don't know how to thank you."

"Just get home safely," Buffy replied. "That's what I plan to do." She realized she was very tired. The woman offered her a ride home, but Buffy told her she just lived down the street.

The woman beeped her horn and sped off into the night.

Buffy was already thinking about other things.

When Gloria had repeatedly mentioned "them," it had reminded Buffy of so much that had gone before.

Vampires didn't simply show up in Sunnydale. They tended to come here in groups. They were attracted by the power of the Hellmouth. The very first big-league vampire that Buffy had to face, the Master, had actually been trapped in the caves around the Hellmouth and had had a plan to use the blood of many mortals to free himself. Of course, destroying the Slayer had also been part of the plan.

Buffy had survived that one—barely. She had actually died for a moment, saved only by Xander's quick thinking and knowledge of CPR.

Once the Master was gone, the next group of vampires moved in, led by a pair of punks named Spike and Drusilla. They were going to destroy the world just because they could. Only the interference of Angel after he lost his soul caused their plans to fail, upsetting the mix and causing the vamps to turn on each other. *Poor Angel.*

Buffy swore she would never get close to a vampire again.

She stopped and listened. There was nothing, at least not yet.

There would be.

Now that the other woman was gone, the tingling was back, the feeling that something was about to strike.

"Slayer!"

The call was faint at first, as if the voice were very

far away. *Maybe,* Buffy thought, *it came from the other side of the grave.*

"Slayer!" A second voice was added to the first, and then a third. "Slayer!"

There were a number of vampires out there, somewhere in the shadows. Buffy guessed that Gloria had made good on her threat and had brought them back with her.

"Slay—er. Slay—er. Slay—er."

It had gone from a call to a chant, a dozen voices all calling her name.

"That's my name!" she called back. "Don't wear it out!" Well, it wasn't very original, but hey, a girl had to say something. It was part of her Slayer style.

Her shout brought some immediate results. She saw movement in the darkness. The vampires were coming out.

"Slay—er! Slay—er! Slay—er!" The chant grew louder and louder, more voices joining with every repetition. How many vampires were out there?

Gloria stepped out into the streetlight, followed by a half-dozen others.

"'Gloria,' she says, 'why don't you move out of the way? Let the nice lady back into her car,' she says. Nobody tells Gloria what to do!"

"Slay—er." The chant rose and fell. "Uh—Slay—er." Now that Gloria had interrupted the chant's rhythm, it had lost most of its energy. Which meant they could lose their focus. Buffy would have seen this as a good sign, if there hadn't been so many vampires.

Besides the six that had shown up right behind Gloria, she noticed another dozen or so emerging from the bushes at the edges of the parking lot. She glanced quickly over her shoulder and saw four or five more walk around the corner that brought her here.

"Slayer!" Gloria began again.

"Slay—er!" a couple of the other replied as they slowly approached.

They were forming a loose circle around her.

"Slay—er! Slay—er! Slay—er!" The chant grew loud again as the ring of vampires approached, tightening like a noose around her neck

"Slay—er! Slay—er! Slay—er!"

This, Buffy thought, *does not look good.*

"Hey! Keep it quiet out there! Some people are trying to sleep!"

The voice came from somewhere—an open window, perhaps—in the condo complex beyond the parking lot. The chanting stumbled again, the vampires startled for an instant.

Buffy hoped that an instant would be all she needed.

She turned and ran three quick steps toward the parking lot's entrance. She spun quickly, aiming a kick at the chest of the vampire in her way. He fell back, startled. The bloodsuckers on either side tried to close ranks, but she had a stake in each hand and drove them into the two nearest vampires.

The two vampires crumbled to dust.

A very satisfying move, Buffy thought. *Now all I need is another dozen moves just like it.*

There was an instant of shocked silence, then all the remaining vampires seemed to scream as one.

"Get her!" Gloria demanded.

It was time for Buffy to boogie. There was a clear space before her and twenty-five vampires behind her.

Another stepped in to block her way. "You're not going—"

She kicked his legs out from under him.

But every second she wasn't on the run meant the other vampires were closer. How could she get away from two dozen of the things? Already, she could see them spreading out, trying to block her escape. Vampires were faster than humans. They were almost as fast as the Slayer. *If they all decide to attack at once—*

Headlights turned on in the far corner of the parking lot. A car engine came to life. Wheels squealed as the dark car came careening forward, scattering vampires from its path.

The car screeched to a halt a foot before Buffy. Three doors opened, and three young men in long robes jumped out. This time, though, their hoods were off their heads.

They were the guys from Wales.

Ian held a large crucifix. Tom and Dave both gripped crossbows.

"Back!" Ian called to the surrounding horde.

The ring of vampires, or what was left of it, just stood there and stared.

"Now!" Ian called.

Dave and Tom both shot wooden bolts from their bows. Each bolt found a target. Two more vampires disintegrated.

The vampires hissed and ran, disappearing back into the bushes from which they'd come.

"You haven't heard the last of little old Gloria!" a voice called from somewhere in hiding.

Buffy stared at Ian. "Were you guys waiting there all along?"

Ian nodded. "We had heard rumors of evil in this part of town. So we decided to have a stakeout—that's the word from your cop shows, right?" He smiled one very nice smile. "Particularly appropriate too, considering the circumstances."

But she wouldn't let his charm get in the way of her growing anger. "Somebody could have gotten killed here. What about that woman those vampires attacked?"

"We were just about to break that up. My uncle wanted to make sure that no other vampires were lurking about. Then, just as we were about to get out of the car, you showed up."

"And?" Buffy prompted. "You wanted the vampires to attack me instead?"

There was a bit of embarrassed silence. She was beginning to tell the three brothers apart, personalitywise. Ian was the serious one, Tom was full of energy, bouncing on the balls of his feet, always ready to go running after something. She guessed that Dave, despite the beard, was the youngest; he was quiet and quick to smile. He looked like he just wanted to be liked.

Dave was the one who finally explained: "My uncle wanted to see just what you could do."

"You did handle yourself very well," Ian added, "until, of course, the vampire population became unmanageable."

So I'm being tested? Who were these people, to make this sort of judgment?

The driver's door of the car opened. An older man, also dressed in a robe, stepped out to regard Buffy.

"Slayer," the older man announced. "We are honored to witness your skill. Excuse our entrance, but we needed to speak with you alone."

Well, she guessed they had saved her life. Hearing them out was the least she could do.

"So talk" Buffy replied.

"All right!" the voice shouted from the window of the complex. "That's it! Enough noise! I'm calling the police!"

The older man glanced back at the condo complex. "I think we might give you a lift, oh—anywhere else than here."

Buffy hesitated only an instant before getting into the front passenger side of the car. They might be strange, even infuriating, but her Slayer sense told her they didn't mean her any harm. The three young men piled in the back.

The older man climbed in behind the wheel and shifted the large car—Buffy thought it was some kind of Cadillac—into drive.

He glanced over to her once they were safely on the road. "I'm glad we finally meet face-to-face. The time for secrecy is over. There are things happening in the Hellmouth that will effect us all."

Chapter 8

THE DRUIDS SPOKE THROUGH THEIR DREAMS.

George had had many experiences with the dream state throughout his life, from the day he was first admitted to the order through his ascension to elder. But his dreams had not always been as vivid as those of his fellows; the message was more vague than he might have liked. If only he could have been more like his brother Stephen, who had truly mastered the art.

George had always found his dreams disappointing, until the day after his brother's death. On that day, he had had the first of the dreams of the hillside. He had had a hundred variations of the dream since. As vivid as these dreams were, he found them beyond exact understanding. In some, his brother was there to help him. In others, Stephen seemed the embodiment of pure evil.

He had thought at first they were nothing but a reaction to the horrible memories of the day of Stephen's death. Perhaps that was so, and the dreams came at first from his own guilt. But the dreams had grown as the days had passed, and he was sure that they wanted to tell him more.

Since he had come to the Hellmouth the dreams were clearer still. George found it difficult to sleep now; the dreams were that disturbing.

He could hide no longer. It was time to address his dreams directly.

At first, Giles's words made no sense to her at all.

"We may just have the program working."

Buffy's mind was, like, totally elsewhere. She felt Giles was speaking some foreign language.

"What? What program, where?"

"That prediction program." Giles actually smiled. "It seems to have narrowed its focus—considerably."

"I'll say," Willow agreed. When Buffy had entered the library a moment before she had found both of them in their usual places, Willow at her terminal, Giles standing with a book in hand. Now that she actually took time to look at both of them, they did seem considerably more relaxed.

"Remember when we had thousands of things that could go wrong in Sunnydale?" Willow continued. She held up a single sheet of paper. "Well, we're now down to three."

Buffy frowned. "Three? Three what?"

"Potential dangers that the Slayer might face in the near future."

"And they all sound real?"

"Well, as real as anything gets around here. No more mutant whales with feet."

"At least not at the moment," Giles added dryly.

Actually, Buffy thought, maybe the stuff she came here for could wait for a minute. This sounded interesting.

"So, there are only *three* things we need to prepare for?"

"Well, yeah," Willow replied, "if we could completely understand them. This computer program might be better, but it's not perfect."

"I'm afraid one of the items is pretty obscure," Giles added.

"Only one?" Willow asked. "Here. Take a look."

She handed the sheet to Buffy, who was surprised to see it held only a half-dozen sentences. She read the first of the three entries aloud:

There is a shift in the undead. There exists a potential for a gathering of vampires.

Willow shook her head. "Well, that's like a no-brainer. In Sunnydale, there is always the potential for a gathering of vamps."

Buffy saw what Willow meant. The next one on the list was already a little enigmatic.

A new wave will sweep the surface clean. Beware of those lurking below.

What did *that* mean?

"I wonder if that's what happened to the computer?" Willow asked. "This so-called new-wave thingie swept it clean."

"It all sounds a bit like ancient myth," Giles added, "the Oracle at Delphi or some such. The program now appears to be giving us not so much specifics as signs and portents that might lead us to the truth. Can we understand them? And, if so, might we believe them?"

"Whatever you say," Buffy agreed. Sometimes, when she was in the computer world of Willow and Giles, she felt like she was out of her depth. Maybe the third entry would clear things up. She read aloud again:

A single night will mean the difference. The power could change everything.

This time, she said it aloud. "What does *that* mean?"

"Unfortunately I think it could mean just about anything," Giles said with a shake of his head. "People have been predicting things like this for years. If it's obscure enough, it has to be true—somewhere."

Buffy waved the paper in the air. "And you say this is better than what we had before?"

"Well, it's certainly more manageable," Giles allowed.

"And even more obscure," Willow added. "I have to figure out why the program did this. Until we have the right questions, what good are the answers?"

"A point well taken," Giles agreed. "However, I thought it worth discussing these possibilities with Buffy, just in case she has had any experiences that might lend credence to our research."

Buffy smiled at her mentor, always using twelve words when two would do.

"It might also show if you're on the right track," she added.

"Indeed," Giles agreed.

"So what you're saying," Willow added, "is that we have to figure out what's changed in Sunnydale recently?"

My cue. This was the very reason she'd come to the library.

"Druids," she announced.

"Beg pardon?" Giles asked.

"Druids," Buffy replied. "There are these new guys in town. Willow met three of them at the Bronze the other night."

"Amanda's cousins?" Willow said. "The guys from Wales."

"Right. Well, last night I saw them again, only this time they were wearing robes, like that guy who helped me out in that vamp attack a few days back? Except this time none of them were wearing hoods, so I could recognize them. They had an older man with them. They said he was their uncle. They knew all about the Slayer, and me being the Slayer. And they said they were Druids."

Giles' eyebrows rose in alarm. "Druids? Did they

tell you anything? Did they make any demands? Any threats?"

Buffy frowned. "No, these are more your friendly neighborhood Druids. Definitely non-threatening. But they're pretty much non-speaking, too. They like to ask questions. They don't like to answer them."

"Well," Giles replied. "I suppose it's possible they're what they say they are. The Druids were believed to have died out completely, some time after the advent of Christianity."

"Well, there are some people who claim to be Druids on the Web," Willow added, "but then there are some people on the Web who claim to be bug-eyed monsters."

"Yuck," Buffy agreed.

"From what little we know," Giles continued, "they were believed to be the priests of ancient Celtic civilizations, highly educated, highly literate, but teaching entirely through oral tradition. If they still exist, I imagine they exist completely independent of modern technology."

Buffy shook her head. "According to the one I talked to last night, not only do they still exist, but they've come to Sunnydale."

Giles frowned. "So now Druids come to the Hellmouth."

Buffy threw up her hands. "Who *doesn't* come to the Hellmouth?"

Xander came striding through the library door.

"Hey, guys, what's up?"

He came to an abrupt halt, glancing around at the serious faces. "Uh-oh. From the looks in this room, I guess something's happening that I probably don't want to know about."

"Druids," Buffy replied

"And computer prophecies," Willow added.

Xander paused for a minute before replying. "Well, maybe later. In the meantime, anybody seen Cordelia?"

Buffy shook her head. Giles said she hadn't been in all day.

"This can mean only one thing," Buffy announced.

Willow and Buffy exchanged looks. They said the next three words together. "The Spring Formal."

"Also known as Xander Wears a Tux," he agreed with a weary smile. "No mystery there."

"All of us have to make sacrifices," Giles agreed

"These Druids," Willow asked, "didn't they make sacrifices?"

"Later!" Xander called as he fled the room.

Giles nodded, continuing in lecture mode as if Xander had not even come in. "Animal sacrifices at the very least. Perhaps even human sacrifices. It all had to do with their religion, which as near as I can figure out from the few writings that do survive from the time, was a highly evolved form of nature worship."

"Writing?" Buffy asked. "But I thought you said

they exchanged all their knowledge by word of mouth." *See, I can pay attention.*

"Indeed they did. But others wrote *of* them, primarily the Romans, who of course were out to conquer their people. Since the Romans might have colored their reportage to make their cause look better, it isn't exactly an unbiased report."

Buffy found herself getting frustrated all over again. "Then how do we—how does anybody, find out about the Druids?"

"Perhaps I can answer your questions."

An older gentleman wearing a business suit strode into the library.

Don't look now, Buffy thought, *it's Uncle Druid.*

Gloria couldn't believe it. Some people acted like they owned the world.

"How dare you!"

They wanted Gloria to grovel, to get down on her hands and knees and beg forgiveness. But Gloria could explain everything. "It wasn't like I went looking for her. Bernie and I were just looking for a meal. Well, I know how you said how we should all work on this together. But sometimes a girl gets hungry, you know?"

She shifted uncomfortably under the other's gaze. "So anyway, there we were, minding our own business, about to suck some nice fresh blood out of a woman maybe twenty—real prime stuff, you know?" Her eyes half closed at the thought. "Um-hmm, I could already taste it." She paused and swallowed. "Oh, sorry, got sidetracked. So there we were, and she barges in. The nerve! She kills Bernie right off. And you should have heard how she talked to me."

"She is the Slayer."

"Don't remind me," Gloria huffed.

"Keep away from the Slayer. I have plans for everyone."

"Well, I can see your point, of course." Whenever somebody talked in short sentences like that, Gloria felt she had to talk to fill in all the silences. "You stepped in when all the big boys went running. Just because there are going to be a few changes around here. They didn't have any nerve at all! We needed somebody to, y'know, show us the way—like, lead us? Me and the others really appreciate it."

"And this is how you show your appreciation?" The voice floated around her, tinged with amusement.

Gloria winced a little. "So I got mad. So I took some of the guys out to beat some sense into the Slayer. Is that such a crime?" Gloria hesitated when she saw the look. "Oh. I guess it is."

"It's not your fault, Gloria. It sometimes takes an outsider to see all the possibilities. Not that I'm going to be an outsider anymore."

"Listen, I never thought—well, what does it matter what I think, huh?" She smiled her friendliest smile. "Oh, yeah, everything's gonna be just fine."

"That's what I want to hear, Gloria. Play along, and I just may let you help destroy the Slayer."

"We're going to destroy the Slayer?"

"We're going to attack her where she is weakest. We're going to destroy her trust."

Gloria clapped her hands. Maybe everything would work out for the best after all.

Chapter 9

THIS HAD TO BE HANDLED MOST DELICATELY.

Rupert Giles stepped between the intruder and the students. There was no guessing the intruder's intentions.

"And you might be?" Giles asked.

The man had graying hair cut slightly long and a neatly trimmed mustache. "Call me George. Miss Summers has already met me." His accent had a slight British lilt, perfectly in keeping with his image. "And, you, I presume, are her Watcher?"

"So you know about us?" Giles supposed he shouldn't be surprised if this fellow was who he thought he was.

"There were Slayers even back in those times when my kind ruled most of Europe. We have always done our best to honor and protect the tradition."

"And you are the leader—"

"Of our small band? I have that honor. I am a priest and elder of our order."

"Druids?"

George smiled affably. "One of our names, the one most commonly known. It will certainly suffice."

Giles regarded the newcomer for a moment. For now, he guessed he would accept him at face value.

"So the Druids never did die out?"

"Certainly not. We just became decidedly less public. We have still passed our knowledge on down through the ages.

"There have always been small cells of us, a few hundred strong, often throughout Europe, sometimes elsewhere. We could not let the way die out, for we knew there would come a time when we would be needed again."

He paused and looked from Giles to Buffy and back again. "That time is now upon us."

Buffy nodded. "You talked about this in the car last night."

"In the car?" Giles asked, ever-so-slightly aghast. Buffy had accepted a ride from this stranger? Most certainly she was the Slayer, but sometimes he thought Buffy had no common sense.

The Druid nodded. "I am sorry if my methods are somewhat abrupt, but we do not have much time. All the information I had at my disposal suggested that Miss Summers was the Slayer. As soon as I determined that was indeed the case, I decided to contact her and then you with all speed so that I might pursue what must be done."

"What must be done?" Giles didn't like someone else marching in here and making demands. Perhaps it came from the past couple of years of dealing with vampires, monsters, and assorted demons, but Giles was very wary of this George.

George appeared to sense Giles's reluctance. "I'm sorry. I'm being impatient now that we are so close. Some explanation is in order." He sighed. "Where to begin? With the Hellmouth, I suppose."

He paused for a moment before he continued, as if he were choosing his words very carefully. "No doubt you are aware that there are certain points of power in the world. Stonehenge might be the most famous example, a temple built by those people who came before the Druids, but used by our priests for many of their rituals for over two thousand years. Through the mysteries of our planet, which even we do not fully understand, these places of power shift in strength and importance. Sometimes, of course, they even are lost to us, such as that place of power that was once the center of Atlantis, now lost far beneath the sea.

"And the shifts continue today. We have noticed the major points of power in Europe have been fading for the last hundred years, replaced in strength by a point in China, another in Africa, and this third one, the Hellmouth, the strongest of them all."

He turned away from Buffy and Giles for a moment to look at the rows and rows of books around them. "This is quite an impressive collection, Mr. Giles. Learned books on many of the great mysteries, including a few, I see, on this very topic. Should we be able to combine your knowledge with our own, we will not fail. But I'm getting ahead of myself."

He turned back to the three in the room, but his eyes no longer seemed to focus on them, instead gazing off into some space far beyond them.

"We detected it first, perhaps a century ago. The delicate balance between man and nature was shifting farther from the center than it ever had been before. To the common man it could be seen in the increased outbursts of violence in our cities and in our homes, the proliferation of serial killers, the never-ending ethnic, religious, and caste wars that seem to spring up all over the globe. All these symptoms could be explained away and might eventually be treated, even eradicated, by modern day means.

"But there is a darker side to this shift in the balance, which you have seen here, and we have seen at other points of power. When the delicate balance of nature is disrupted, darker things emerge. Our ancient stories talk about the ten thousand demons, waiting to emerge from the other side."

"Ten thousand demons?" Giles vaguely remembered reading something about that in one of the early versions of their not-quite-perfect computer program—something about a particular demon who specialized in eating eyes.

George cleared his throat, as if surprised by the interruption. "I do not know if that is literally true," he replied. "Any oral tradition, even our own, will elaborate over the course of time. But whatever their true nature, the supernatural forces will attempt to reassert their dominion over the Earth—a dominion they enjoyed before the Druids drove them out nearly five thousand years ago."

"Five thousand years?" Buffy asked.

George allowed himself the faintest of smiles. "A long time for you and me. A heartbeat for the forces of evil."

He looked again to the three in the room. "The elders of my order came to realize that if something were not done quickly to shift the balance closer to its natural course, the forces of darkness would be freed again to rule the world.

"Alas, we tried to change the balance at one of the old points of power, too far away from the source. It was a foolish miscalculation. This spell would effect the whole world. Therefore, it must be conducted at the world's strongest point.

"The spellcasting was a disaster. Some of you have met my nephews. It was in attempting this spell that the boys' father met his death. The point of power was not strong enough. It is only then that the elders realized that in order to succeed, we had to seek out the strongest mystic point on the entire face of the earth."

He paused for an instant before adding:

"Only by using the Hellmouth might we drive back the forces of evil and save the world."

He smiled then. "That's why we're here, my nephews and I. I have the necessary knowledge. My nephews may lack experience, but they are young and strong, willing to face up to the task ahead. Even we are not certain of all the signs. This may be our last opportunity."

"Maybe this is what the prophecy means!" Willow piped up.

George frowned. "What do you mean—prophecy?"

"Just an experiment my students and I are conducting," Giles replied curtly. The Druid's words certainly sounded plausible. But Giles still wanted to know a lot more about their plans before he shared any facts of his own.

"Well, not the one about the vampires," Willow continued, apparently oblivious to Giles's concerns. "But this one, maybe: 'A new wave will sweep the surface clean. Beware of those lurking below.'"

George frowned. There was a long moment of silence.

"Interesting," he said at last. "What do you think it means?"

"I was hoping you could tell us," Willow replied, "you being a Druid and all."

George shook his head. "Prophecy has always been a part of the Druidic art. Unfortunately, it is an inexact art, and one in which I am not well versed."

He paused again, as if listening to something that Giles could not hear. "We will have to talk again. Now, there are things I must do."

He nodded to each of the three before him. "The things we fight have been hidden by the rush to technology from much of the rest of the world. Here, on the Hellmouth, there is no ignoring these changes. You see them every day.

"Certainly you have noticed the extreme amount of activity—the ever greater prevalence of pure evil. We are here to stop it, before it is too late.

"There are those who are determined to stop us, for we would tip the balance once more, banishing their kind of terror from the earth.

"In ancient times, the priests and the Slayer worked side by side, I was hoping we might do so again.

"But I have already taken too much of your time. I will give you time to discuss this. I imagine, should you go to the Bronze tonight, you will find my nephews. Tell them if you wish to speak further."

The Druid took a single step away from them. Shadows seemed to swirl around him, shadows cast by nothing Giles could see. In an instant, he was enveloped by darkness. Then the darkness faded, and he was gone.

His final words echoed in the air. "Remember, we must act soon."

Both Willow and Buffy gasped.

Willow said it first. "He's using magic!"

"I could have told you that," Giles snapped. *No,*

he thought, *no need to take out your anxiety on the young women.* He took a deep breath, then added, "They are very strict about letting unauthorized outsiders into schools these days."

"So he just popped into existence," Buffy asked, choosing not to remind her Watcher of the demons, vampires, assasins, and ghosts that had walked the school halls recently, "right in this room?"

"If he was ever truly here at all. I believe we were speaking with some form of astral projection, something I would think would be perfectly in keeping with Druidism."

Giles sighed. If only he could trust these Druids. He might finally have true allies in the fight against darkness. But earlier battles had left him cautious. And there was something about George. Not his reserve—no, Giles was reserved. He expected that in a certain sort of man. George seemed secretive, like he was presenting a well-rehearsed speech that hid some portion of his plan.

"Still," he added to the others, "I feel he wasn't telling us everything he knew."

"You know," Willow remarked, *"he's* the new thing in Sunnydale. I wonder if the Druids' arrival had anything to do with the changes in the computer program?"

Giles hadn't thought of that. "Whether everything left because of *them?* That's a little extreme, isn't it?"

"Wait a minute!" Buffy jumped in. "Look at the second prediction. 'A new wave will sweep the surface clean. Beware of those lurking below.' It might apply to them."

"You mean the Druids are the new wave?"

"Quite possibly," Giles agreed. "Did you see the way he hesitated when Willow read him that? I believe he knew something that might make sense out of the second prediction."

These Druids are a new *wave? Well, they are in Sunnydale. It could fit,* Giles thought. It still didn't help them interpret the third prediction:

"A single night will mean the difference. The power could change everything."

This Druid had certainly talked about power. This last prediction could very possibly be a warning. But was it a warning against Druids, or the things they were here to overcome?

"What to do?" Giles said aloud.

"Well, George isn't the only Druid in town," Buffy replied. "And his three nephews seem a bit more 90's."

"Definitely more 90's," Willow agreed. "Not to mention friendly."

"Almost like real people." Buffy grinned. "I think it's time to follow up on Uncle George's suggestion and get jiggy with some Druids!"

"Jiggy?" Giles asked. Sometimes, Buffy's nomenclature left him at a loss.

"We'll tell you what we find out at the Bronze," Willow interpreted.

Chapter 10

Xander was amazed at how much they had to talk about. Here they were, he and Oz from Sunnydale, USA, and three guys from some unpronounceable town in Wales, of all places. But they could talk about things that most other people in Sunnydale wouldn't even dream of. Vampires, werewolves, Incan mummies—these three guys just accepted these things. What a relief it was to finally be able to talk openly about this stuff. Just a bunch of guys hanging at the Bronze, who had to face the supernatural every day. Xander thought he could get into this sort of thing.

Ian had just finished telling a story of a particularly nasty demon they had helped their father with. All four of them had to write the proper mystical symbols, each one of the four slightly different, and in the proper sequence, in order to banish the creature from this physical plane.

"Sounds sort of like playing in a rock band," Oz said. "The drummer pounds, the bass guy plunks, the lead guitar's got your power chords, and then the singer brings in the words. Hey, you've got a song."

"Yes, it was rather like that," Ian agreed.

"Our father was very good at incantations," Tom added with a sad smile. "That's the thing that finally banished the creature."

"It was one of the best I've ever heard," Dave said, quietly echoing the sentiment. "It's . . ." Dave turned away. He was very still. Xander wondered what it would be like to lose a father. He decided to leave the joke book out of it for now.

"You were very proud of your father?" Xander asked.

"Oh, certainly that," Tom agreed. The three brothers glanced at each other. Dave still looked like he was about to break down in tears. "He taught us just about everything. But our father was always very gifted—perhaps the most gifted—among our order in using the mystic arts. He'd be able to handle this Hellmouth thing in a snap."

"Hey!" Xander blurted. These guys were assuming an awful lot. Buffy and the gang had to work full time just to keep Sunnydale standing. "The Hellmouth isn't exactly Sesame Street!"

Tom shuffled his feet. "No, but then Big Bird wasn't a Druid, either."

"Our Uncle George, you see," Ian cut in. "He certainly means well, and with the proper preparation, he'll get the job done."

"He's very methodical," Tom answered.

"Just not very inspired." Dave took a deep breath and finished the thought. "But until we come of age, he is our leader, and we'll stand behind him."

The three young men nodded in unison.

Ian leaned over the table to look at Oz and Xander. "That's another reason we might need your help. You don't have our training, but you do have practical experience."

"Practical experience?" Xander laughed. "I guess that's one way to put it on a resume." When he thought of all his experiences with vampires and demons and giant snakes, he considered it more like "just barely surviving."

"So, is there anything else you'd like to know?" Ian asked.

Xander thought for a moment before he replied. "According to Buffy, when your uncle showed up at the library, he talked a lot, but he didn't say all that much."

"Oh, that's our Uncle George. He just likes to be mysterious."

"Do you know anything about lycanthropy!" Oz called over the din. With the loud music at the Bronze, one could shout and still not be overheard.

"Lycanthropy?" Ian replied. "I believe so. We'd have to ask our uncle. It's one of the more common curses. I think some of those back home are skilled in the tradition."

Oz shook his head. "No, I don't want to make somebody a werewolf. I want to *unmake* one."

"All part of the same spell—I think." Tom grinned as if he couldn't wait to try it.

"We haven't quite reached that in our lessons," Dave admitted.

Xander hadn't even thought about the possibilities of Druidic power. "Wow, you're sort of like a superstore of spells, huh?"

"You want to be unmade?" Tom asked Oz.

"Well, maybe we could do that, or maybe not," Oz agreed. "It's tough. It's one of the things that makes me me if you know what I mean."

Xander guessed that he did.

"Still," Oz added, "I wouldn't mind being able to get out of the house on nights with a full moon, and not spend all my time growling and trying to eat small animals."

Xander couldn't relate to that quite so directly. Well, actually, he *had* been turned into a hyena once. Were hyenas that different from wolves? Anyway, he could still see Oz's point.

Suddenly Buffy leaned past Xander and smiled at all the guys around the table. Xander always thought Buffy looked good, but tonight she looked fabulous, with a dark jacket and fairly low-cut blouse showing off both her fair skin and blond hair.

"Hey, guys," she called, "what are you all laughing about?"

Ian shrugged, not quite looking her in the face. "Oh, we're just telling your friends here some boring old stories about our homeland."

"Hey," Xander cut in, "don't let them kid you. Some of the supernatural stuff they've faced is right up there in Slayersville."

"Oh, I wouldn't—," Ian started to say.

"Well, I'm hanging over there with Willow and Amanda." Buffy pointed at a table a few feet away. "I was thinking maybe later we could all get together?"

Before Xander could tell Buffy to bring the others on over, Ian said, "Well, maybe . . . later."

What is the problem with this guy? Xander wondered. First, he grabbed Xander and Oz before they could meet up with their gang. Now he wouldn't even let Buffy and the others join them. Did Ian have a thing about girls? Xander was half-tempted to stand right up and march over to Buffy's table. He would, too, as soon as Ian and the others stopped sharing all their Druidic secrets.

"Oh." Buffy gave a little wave. "Okay. See ya."

What could Xander say back but "See ya"?

He turned to Ian as soon as she'd left. "Is it always that cold in Wales?"

Ian looked down at the table. "Oh, she's the Slayer. She wouldn't be interested in any of this."

"Buffy's nobody to be scared of," Xander replied. "She may be the Slayer, but she's regular people."

"Regular," Oz agreed.

A familiar voice called over his shoulder. "Hey, Xander. Here I am!"

Xander looked up. It was Cordelia. *I've been looking for her all day. She finally shows up now?*

"You guys look tight," Cordelia said. "Listen, I'll just go sit over there with Amanda and the others."

Xander knew that Cordelia really wanted him to invite her to join them. Only, right this second, he didn't feel like it.

"Listen," he replied instead. "I'll come over in a minute. OK?"

"Uh—OK." Cordelia smiled and waved. "Nice seeing you guys."

Now, Xander guessed, he was giving *her* the cold shoulder. But he was getting pretty annoyed with her, too. These last couple of days, it seemed every time she had promised to spend time with him, she ended up disappearing.

Ian smiled when Cordelia left. He seemed more comfortable when the women were gone. He smacked his hands loudly on the table.

"Here, we don't have all night. I promised to show you a couple of little tricks."

Cordelia stared over at the table filled with young men, her own Xander among them. Little puffs of smoke were rising from the middle of the table. Cigarettes weren't allowed in the Bronze, but maybe Amanda's cousins didn't know that.

She nodded to Buffy and Willow. Amanda sat at

the table, too, but she was busy talking to Becky Grimes at the next table over.

Willow glanced back at the animated male conversation. "So what are they so busy talking about?"

"Boy," Cordelia complained, "I leave to talk about the Spring Formal for what—fifteen or twenty minutes—and Xander gets lost in this other conversation. It's like he barely knows I'm here."

Buffy sighed. "You know, Cordelia, Xander might have been feeling a little neglected."

"Neglected? Do you think so? He has to realize the importance of this event." She shook her head in wonder. "We only have a few more major dances before we graduate!"

Willow grinned. "Dances, wow. Oz is always playing at dances. Which is cool and all, but sometimes a girl would like to dance, sort of. How about you, Buffy?"

"Dance?" Buffy sighed. "I'm the Slayer. Case closed."

Cordelia glanced back at the guy table. Xander was obviously ignoring her. But one of the newcomers, the cutest of the three, in Cordelia's opinion, kept stealing glances their way.

Cordelia leaned across the table. "Buffy, you see the way one of the new guys looks at you?"

"You mean Ian?" Buffy asked, straightening a little and adjusting her jacket. "Well, yeah, I thought I noticed. I'm kind of out of practice." She sighed one more time. "I thought I saw him look; once I even caught him smiling. But then every time I get near him, he turns around and has a conversation with somebody else."

Typical, Cordelia thought. "Well, he *is* a male."

"Always a difficulty," Willow agreed.

"And I'm the Slayer. It's an automatic turnoff."

It was Cordelia's turn to be exasperated. She had never known the girl to be so dense. "Buffy! You're the Slayer, this guy's a Druid! It's a match made, if not in heaven, at least in Sunnydale! I mean, the guy's not *my* type, but you might be perfect for each other."

"You think so?"

"Hey, it's worth a try. Look at him. He's got a cute smile and those really intense blue-gray eyes. Not that I noticed. And that curly dark hair. And, and—"

"And he's mysterious!" Willow added.

"Well, yeah," Buffy admitted. "I do like mysterious."

"Maybe a little too much," Cordelia added, remembering Angel. *Now there's someone who's lying low these days. Wonder what he's up to?* "But, hey, what would it hurt to talk to him?"

"Maybe he won't talk to you because he's a Druid," Willow suggested.

"What do you mean?" Buffy asked.

"Well, who knows?" Willow said. "Druids and Slayers may be forbidden to meet by the Druid code or something."

"The Druid code?" Buffy thought about that for a moment. "It's probably that their uncle doesn't want them getting too friendly with anybody."

Cordelia didn't think it was that at all. "Well, they're getting friendly with the guys." She glared at Xander's back.

"You know what I mean," Willow insisted. "They can probably only date other Druids."

"You think so?" Buffy asked. "Maybe their uncle makes them be unsocial. . . ."

"I could buy the uncle thing," Willow admitted. "The guys are cute. The uncle's a little creepy."

"Now what?" Cordelia demanded. The boys at the other table had all stood up and were moving toward the front door of the Bronze. "They're going to leave without saying goodbye?"

"It's probably a Druid thing," Willow ventured again.

"What makes you say that?"

"Well, Oz is pretty fascinated by all their spells and stuff. He told me maybe they could do something about the werewolf business. So I'm trying to be understanding, when they turn around and leave and don't even say a word. . . ." Willow did not look at all understanding.

The group of boys laughed as they headed for the door to leave the club.

"Well, I don't care at all." Cordelia looked around the club. There must be something, or someone, else interesting in this place.

"Well, I do." Willow announced. "What if they do

something—you know, Druidic? Don't you want to see?"

"Hey," Buffy joined in. "Just because they've put up their No Chicks Allowed sign doesn't mean we have to agree."

Willow nodded. "Girl power."

"I'm not—" Cordelia paused and looked at the other two. If they were going to be stood up for some stupid magic, she wanted to see, too. She stood up. "Let's go."

The three of them quickly followed the boys' path.

"Cordy!" Amanda called from the table behind them. "We still haven't talked about the decorations!"

"Later!" she called over her shoulder. A young woman had to have her priorities.

The street outside was deserted.

For a moment, Buffy couldn't figure out where the guys had gone. Then she heard faint laughter around the corner.

"Come on." She waved for the others to follow. "We're about to sneak a peek at the boys' club."

The three of them stopped short at the corner. The street in front of them was full of flowers.

They could hear voices drifting from just out of sight.

"Maybe we can give you an hour before school," Xander was saying.

"After school," Oz added, "we've got plenty of time."

Willow looked to her friends. "We've lost them forever."

"To a bunch of Druids?" Cordelia made a face and kicked at the nearest flowers, which appeared to be growing through the concrete. "Its like they're all attending sorcery shop!"

"Sorcery shop?" Willow asked.

"You know, like metal shop, but with magic!"

"Hey," Willow said, "that's pretty good. But why did they have to come out here?"

"Besides the fact that somebody would have noticed all the flowers growing all over the Bronze?" Cordy asked.

"Maybe they just spend all their time around magic," Buffy surmised, "and they're not that comfortable around girls." She remembered with a pang how Kendra, in full Slayer mode, hadn't known how to act around Xander.

"So they know the secrets of the ages but they can't ask anybody out on a date?" Willow asked. "What's with that?"

Cordelia shrugged.

Males lacking social skills? Buffy thought. That they could all understand.

"Maybe they don't have any women in the Druids," Cordy ventured.

"No," Buffy replied. "They'd have to. Otherwise, how could they have baby Druids?" She knelt to pick a flower. It felt real enough and smelled divine, but already the street looked less like a garden and more streetlike. *Are they fading? Was it an illusion?* She gripped her stem a little tighter.

Willow shook her head. "I actually looked this up after Uncle George showed up. The Druids were anything but a men-only club. They had both priests and priestesses. You know, many early religions were woman centered, based on the worship of the Goddess—you know, like Mother Earth. I read one theory that said Druidism might be a direct descendent of these religions."

It figured. Cordelia had pegged these three newcomers as boring from the start. "So this No Chicks Allowed thing isn't the Druids. It's just them."

"Maybe they're just trying to be—extra mysterious," Buffy mused.

"Well, if they are, I think it's working," Cordelia pointed out. "Who have we been talking about ever since we came out here?"

"I think they're just being extra annoying. Especially Ian." Buffy had had enough of this. The flowers were gone. Except the one in her hand. The street was back to plain, unbroken asphalt, as if the flowers had never been there in the first place. She turned around and headed back toward the club.

She heard the others talking as she marched away.

Cordelia said "She likes him."

Willow replied "That's a definite yes."

Sometimes her friends could be so infuriating.

Especially when they were right.

* * *

"So, yeah," Ian said. "If you can help us, we'll do our best to help you."

Xander thought these guys were all right. "Actually, I wouldn't mind learning that flower trick."

"I think it would definitely help if we formed an alliance here," Ian continued. "I mean, not that we're going to be in town long or anything. But we can work together as long as we're here."

"So you could give us basic Druid lessons?" Xander asked. "If that's okay. I don't want to step on anybody's toes."

"My Uncle George would probably be ticked off if he knew we were talking this much to you," Tom added. "He said we should try to keep to ourselves."

"So why aren't you with him?" Oz asked, leaning against a non-working phone stand. They'd come outside to see the flower trick and Dave was grabbing a quick cigarette. From the way his brothers glared at him, Oz figured Dave would be kicking the habit quite soon.

"He's still preparing things. At this point we'd just be in the way."

"We have to keep a certain distance," Dave said between drags. "At least according to our uncle. After all, we're Druids."

Ian sighed. "Our father was a lot looser. Uncle George is stricter, more old guard. But we know he'll do a good job."

"It's important to all of us," Tom agreed. "Because our father died as a part of this, we feel we need to finish the job. I guess it's our father's legacy."

Dave nodded. "And we're going to need as much help as we can get."

"Including the Slayer?" Xander asked.

"Especially the Slayer," Ian agreed.

"You know, we've been hanging out here, having a good time," Oz said. "We've sort of been neglecting the girls."

"Sort of?" Xander replied. "We completely left them out of the loop." *And,* he thought, *I did it because I was mad at Cordelia.*

"Well, why don't we go and put them back in." Oz looked at Ian. "You guys, too."

"Well," Ian replied, "if you think so."

They marched back into the Bronze.

Willow smiled at them from the table where all the girls had been before. She sat on one side of the table, while Amanda was at the other end, deep in conversation with a girl from the next table.

There was no sign of Buffy—or Cordelia.

Xander couldn't believe it. *Where did that girl go now?*

Chapter 11

JOYCE SUMMERS WOKE WITH A START.

She had been dreaming. Something about her daughter. It only made sense. She had been sitting in the living room, unable to sleep, waiting for Buffy to come in the door. She was half-watching some awful made-for-TV movie where a fortyish woman had discovered her husband had at least three other wives and was a supposed serial killer. Joyce wished her problems were as simple as that.

Her dream had been disturbing. She could still hear Buffy's voice.

"Mother. Don't you understand?"

She saw her daughter, flanked by a group of men in dark robes. Most of the men seemed friendly. But one of them was not friendly. One of them was not what he seemed. One of them meant to do Buffy harm.

"Mother. Don't you understand?"

That's what the dream was trying to tell her. That she had to understand, to somehow warn Buffy. Joyce could never remember a dream that was quite this vivid. She wondered if it had anything to do with her learning that her daughter was—the Chosen One. If her daughter had special powers, maybe Joyce had one or two as well.

But if that were true, it would be even more important to figure out the dream.

"Mother. You don't understand."

The dark men—did they have anything to do with the boy Buffy had just met? Her daughter could certainly take care of herself under most ordinary circumstances, but this dream did not feel at all ordinary.

She heard the key turn in the front door, then heard the door swing open.

"Buffy?"

"Yeah, Mom. I thought I'd come home a little early for a change."

This is early? No, Joyce told herself, *you don't want to start an argument.* "I'm glad you're home," she said instead. "Do anything interesting?"

Buffy poked her head in the room. "Just went to the Bronze." She did not look at all happy.

"Was that boy you were interested in there?"

Buffy hesitated, as if it was all too personal. "Well, yeah. Not that he'd talk to me."

Joyce had a hunch. "Does this boy have anything to do with—dark robes?"

"Psychic Friends Network." Buffy stared at her mother. "Well, yeah Mom. Kind of. It's part of this kind of . . . club he's in. How'd you know?"

Joyce shook her head. "I just had the funniest dream. Well, it wasn't funny at all. I think it was more of a warning. There was something about these men in dark robes. It seemed dangerous."

"Well, Mom, as of tonight, I think the chances of me getting involved with that guy are as great as me burning down another high school."

Joyce frowned.

"No way would I ever burn down another high school," Buffy quickly added. "We're staying in Sunnydale forever, even if I never meet another eligible guy. Which I won't."

"Oh," her mother replied. Buffy's head disappeared, and she heard her daughter clomp upstairs. Joyce guessed, if she cut through her daughter's melodrama, this was good news. What had Buffy called it? The Psychic Friends Network? Maybe Joyce *did* have a few special abilities of her own.

But wait a minute. Why was her daughter going out with men in dark robes?

"I knew you'd come if I called."

She did? Then why didn't I know? Like where am I? And who's talking to me?

Cordelia found herself in the alley behind the Bronze. How had she gotten here? A minute ago, she had been chatting with Buffy and Willow and Amanda, getting a bit annoyed that Xander could spend so much time with three guys from Wales. And then?

"Welcome back, Cordelia."

A single look, and Cordelia remembered.

"Naomi," she whispered. It all came flooding back to her. The flowing gown that covered her feet so that it looked like she floated rather than walked. The perfect, unlined face, so much paler than it had been in life.

This was the face she had seen in the locker mirror, the voice she'd heard crawling along her spine.

Cordelia knew exactly what she had become.

"You're a vampire."

"Only one of my many new talents." Naomi smiled. She didn't display her fangs—yet. Vampires could look quite normal when they wanted to—until they came in for the kill. Then their true bestial natures came out, their eyes glowing red, their mouths filled with fangs. Cordelia shivered. Thanks to Buffy's crowd, she knew far more about vampires than she had ever wanted to.

Naomi floated even closer. Cordelia tried to back away, but she found she was frozen in place. *Just like the other night. How could I have forgotten?*

Naomi stretched out her hand and stroked Cordelia's cheek. Her touch felt like the inside of a freezer.

"I'm a very special vampire, Cordelia. I do think it's so important to keep up appearances."

She smiled again. This time, Cordelia thought she saw the slightest hint of fang.

"Dear Cordelia, elected to the head of the cheerleading squad—over me. Cordelia who dated Bryce Abbot when I longed to go out with him."

What? Bryce Abbot? Cordelia hadn't thought about him in years. "The quarterback? He was a jerk. He couldn't do anything unless he had a football in his hands."

"Quiet, Cordelia!" Naomi actually hissed. But a moment later, she smiled. "It's my time now. This isn't the Spring Formal where you were named Queen—over me!"

Cordelia frowned. "Naomi. You definitely have some issues."

This time, Naomi laughed. Cordelia decided she liked the hissing better.

"Not as many as you're going to have," Naomi said all too sweetly. "I want to share something with you. Come here, my pet! Come here or Naomi will be angry!"

Cordelia heard something moving around the pile of trash on the far side of the alley.

"This is where he lives now," Naomi says. "It's all he deserves."

The thing shambled out from behind the dumpster. Cordelia could think of no other way to describe it. It looked like it once might have been human—if it hadn't been so stooped over, it might have been six feet tall. And those filthy rags hanging from its form might once, long ago, have been clothes. And all of it—the matted hair, the mud-caked flesh, the sodden rags—was the same brown as dead leaves.

"There are so many things I can do to you, dear Cordelia. That's why I'd like to introduce you to one of my creations. But, of course, you two have met before." She waved to the thing. "Stand closer so dear Cordelia can get a good look at you." Naomi giggled. "Now, Cordelia! I'd like you to say hello to an old friend."

Old friend?

The thing growled, showing the remains of a half-dozen yellow-brown, rotted teeth. *What? Who?*

"Cordelia, you disappoint me. You'd never forget an old boyfriend, would you? Dear girl, meet what's left of Brycie Abbot."

Cordelia didn't even want to think of this. This shambling monstrosity—it could have been the same size as Bryce, she guessed. That is, if the star quarterback walked hunched over, if his hands had turned to claws, and if he hadn't taken a shower in a year and a half. *Come to think of it, hadn't Bryce graduated last year? I thought he left for college—*

"Brycie and I went out for a while," Naomi purred, "after you broke up. It was never right though, knowing you had been there before me."

The thing moaned piteously. It shambled a step closer. Cordelia swallowed a scream.

"And then he had the nerve to break up with me!" Naomi's eyes glowed red. "I was so upset, I didn't care if I lived or died. And then I met a vampire."

She held a hand out toward the monstrosity before her. "Oh Brycie, my Brycie. We'll be together for ever and ever. Or at least we will until he rots away. You see, he's still alive, more or less."

The creature growled again.

One thought kept playing in Cordy's brain. *If Naomi can turn Bryce Abbot into this, what is she going to do to me?*

"No talking back, now," Naomi said to the muck thing. "I can pay special attention to you, Brycie!"

The thing took a shambling step away.

"That's one of the perks of being undead," Naomi said brightly. "I know so many ways to cause people pain. I have extra special ways to hurt my little creature here. Brycie will do anything to keep that from happening.

"Dear, dear Cordelia." Naomi turned back to her again. This time she took Cordelia's face in both her dead, cold hands. "If you ever disappoint me, why, I don't even have to bite you. Not that I might, eventually. It would be so pleasant to end your life the way you destroyed mine."

Cordelia couldn't help herself. She just didn't understand. "Destroyed?" she whispered.

Naomi laughed. "You remember all the times you won and I came in second? Well, I became a vampire first, and I'm going to make you pay!

"I'll change you, Cordelia, so no one will ever recognize you again. But first I'll give you to Bryce for a while. I'm sure he'd like to get better acquainted again."

The creature became very animated at this suggestion, lifting its clawed hands above its head and letting out with a howl.

"And who says Naomi doesn't take care of her special friends? Now be a good little creature, Brycie. Go back into the shadows where you belong."

Naomi turned away from her, watching as the thing that had once been Bryce Abbot stumbled back toward his hiding place. Now that her attention was elsewhere, Cordelia tried—really tried—to move away, but she was still frozen in place. Somehow, Naomi allowed Cordelia to talk and to feel the vampire's frozen hands, and nothing more.

"My," Naomi said as the creature vanished among the garbage. "Wasn't that special." She turned back to Cordelia. "Since we're going to be working together, I'll introduce you to another member of our little entourage." She clapped her hands. "Get out here! Now!"

A small woman appeared from the shadows at the far end of the alley. She looked vaguely familiar, like Cordelia had seen her around school at some time. Except now she had the ridged forehead and mouth full of teeth of a vampire looking for blood.

"I'll do whatever they say, now," she mumbled through her fangs. "Gloria won't cause any more trouble. Even for Naomi."

"You remember Gloria." For some reason Cordelia assumed vampires usually tended to look cool and glamorous. She guessed it had something to do with attracting their prey. Cordelia also guessed that

Gloria looked better than she had in life, too. But with Gloria, even the glamour was mousy.

"Actually, no." Cordelia frowned. "Were you in gym class with me, maybe?

" 'Was I in gym class?' she asks. 'No, she doesn't remember me,' she says!" She bared her fangs as she approached. "Well, Gloria will make sure pretty little Cordelia remembers—"

"Gloria," Naomi commanded. "Shut up."

Gloria stopped abruptly and looked at the ground.

Naomi sighed as she looked back at Cordelia. "Sorry. Good help is so hard to find. That's why I've recruited you."

Oh. Gross with a cherry on top. Now Cordelia remembered this girl. "Did you used to chew gum?"

"Yeah," Gloria replied, not looking at either of the others. "You can't do that any more with fangs."

"Junior High. It *was* gym class."

"I could never climb the ropes," Gloria muttered. "But Cordelia was really good at it!"

What, does everybody in Sunnydale have a grudge against me?

"Dear Cordelia. I can't watch you all the time. But Gloria will at night. And during the day, Brycie will never be very far away. They'll tell me if you don't obey.

"In the meantime, Naomi has other plans with the new rulers of this town."

A great wind sprang up. Naomi, laughing, seemed to fly down the alley and out of sight.

"I hate when she does that," Gloria said to

Cordelia. "Naomi's so full of herself. 'Good help is hard to find,' she says. What makes her so special?" She dusted off her clothes. "I'm not so bad to look at."

Well, Cordelia reasoned, *if you could do a total makeover—lose the torn and ratty outfit, comb out her hair, give her face a little color—well, anything was possible—*

"I never had any luck with men," Gloria whined. "Then Gloria finally found a real looker. Of course he was a vampire."

She smiled up at Cordelia. "You'll like dealing with Gloria. You'll see. Gloria's an easygoing sort. Naomi can be a real pain."

"Can I now?"

Cordelia still couldn't move her head, but she recognized Naomi's voice before the vampire floated back into her line of sight.

"Awwww! Gloria doesn't like things sneaking up on her."

"Gloria won't like a lot of things I can do to her." Naomi smiled. "My business didn't take very long at all."

She shook her head, getting her glorious curls to bounce lightly. "I just wanted to see how you two got along." She looked straight at Gloria. "I just wanted to make sure I could trust you."

Naomi turned her attention back to Cordelia. "You won't remember this. You won't remember me at all, until the next time you bring me my dinner.

"Your dinner? What do you—"

"Who are you going out with these days, Cordelia? I'm sure he'd be very tasty."

What? Cordelia thought. *No! Xander!*

"It's going to be so much fun destroying every little bit of your life," Naomi continued, "all your friends, everything you care about."

Cordelia had had enough of this. She didn't care if she was frozen in place. "I'll—I'll get away. I'll never talk to you again. I'll—"

"No, Cordelia dear, I already have you under my spell. Besides, how can you fight something that you can't remember? You'll go on from day to day, wondering where your friends have disappeared to, where your boyfriend has gone, why your pets don't come home. You'll never remember when I give you my commands. But it will be you, Cordelia, who led every one of them to their deaths."

Cordelia felt like she was going to cry. Why was Naomi being so horrible? Was it Cordelia's fault she got to be head of the cheerleaders, went out with all the popular guys, was picked first at all the dances?

"Don't worry, Cordelia. I'll let you remember it all before I kill you."

Naomi was always competitive—even back in their cheerleading days. Could Cordelia help it if she was the better cheerleader?

But Cordelia wouldn't cry. Naomi was horrible now because she was a vampire. It went with the territory. And Cordelia wouldn't give this creature the satisfaction of knowing she was causing her pain.

Someone would save her. *Where is Xander when I need him? Where is Miss Slayer?*

"It's time for me to go. But don't worry. I'll never be very far."

Naomi drifted away from Cordelia until she, too, was lost in the shadows.

Cordelia blinked.

What was she doing in the alley behind the Bronze?

She must have come out here to get some air. Probably because she was so annoyed with Xander.

She felt a chill. *That's what I get,* she supposed, *for running away from my problems.* She'd get Xander to talk to her, one way or another.

That girl, walking down the alley—Cordelia swore she recognized her from junior high gym class.

Oh well, all sorts came to the Bronze. They let anyone in these days.

Well, she may have wandered out here in a daze, but that didn't mean she had to stay out here. Something moved over in the garbage. *Ugh. There are probably rats back here.*

Cordelia turned around and marched back into the Bronze.

Right now, she really needed to see Xander smile.

Chapter 12

"When I grow up, I want to be a Druid," Xander announced.

Oz regarded Xander with a look that was as close as Oz ever came to surprise.

"I just wanted to hear the way it sounds," Xander confessed. "Doctor? Lawyer? Indian chief? Not for me. I'm going to be a Druid!"

"I know how you feel." *Especially,* Oz thought, *if the Druids could give me any way to control, or even cure, that full-moon habit of mine.* He spent a moment studying the spines on the bookcase across the way. They'd come to the library to ask Giles for advice. It was a good quiet place to talk, too. No chance of other kids coming in *here.*

"Well," Oz said at last, "it sounds like they have a lot going for them. And I liked their little magic tricks. I think I'd need something a lot bigger than flowers, though. I've always pretty much accepted it—I'm a werewolf." He glanced at Xander. "You know, Willow and I have never been able to look at a full moon together. I tell you, it's a real downer in the romance department.

"So—with this whole werewolf thing—I could see me getting tight with the Druids. But what about you?"

Xander had obviously considered this long and hard. "Buffy's my best friend. And what can I do to help her? Most of the time, bupkis, nada, the big goose egg, double-oh-seven without the seven on the end. Nothing. If I could only learn a few of the tricks and techniques these guys have, I could back her up when all those beasties show."

Well, that sounded like a pretty good reason to Oz, too. But he still had questions. "What do we really know about these guys? They talk a lot, but they haven't shown us all that much. And we haven't even met the uncle."

"According to Buffy, he's one sour character. Maybe you can only become a full-fledged Druid after you take a sour test. Maybe that's why his three nephews are trying to cram in all that fun. I never thought of it that way."

Oz wanted to review the facts. "But figuring, besides being sour, the Druids are okay . . ."

"Yeah?" Xander asked.

"So I want to walk around under the full moon and you want to be Buffy's sidekick in danger."

"Yeah," Xander agreed.

"So how do we do it?"

"I suppose we keep talking to them."

"Yeah, talking's pretty safe. You know, for all the stuff they've told us, we still don't really know exactly why they're here."

"A very good observation," a cultured voice said behind them.

They both spun around. Giles regarded them both with a slight smile from behind the librarian's desk. When had he walked in here?

"I surmise you did come in here to see me? This is the library, and since I see no booklike objects in your hands, then you must be looking for me."

"Yeah, Giles," Xander said. "We did a lot of talking with the younger Druids last night."

"And they told us," Oz added, "well, they want to do some big thing to stop this evil stuff. But that was pretty much all we got out of it."

"Yeah," Xander added with a grimace, like he hated how nada it sounded. "Well, they seemed like nice guys."

"Except for the uncle. We haven't met the uncle."

"Well, you know, he could be sour, and nice too. In a sour sort of way."

"Their uncle told me much the same thing," Giles agreed. "I've been thinking about this. Druids were believed to have been wiped out in the early days of Christianity. Instead, apparently, they went into hiding for two thousand years. They may have used their secrecy down through the years to protect themselves. But their secrecy is getting in the way now. If someone isn't totally open and honest with me, I suspect the worst."

"The worst?" Oz asked. "What could be the worst?"

"You live above the Hellmouth and you ask that?" Xander asked in return.

Even Giles cracked a bit of a smile at that. Then he sobered. "They talk about working with the Slayer. I'm afraid they might want to *use* the Slayer instead."

The librarian tapped his long fingers on the top of the railing. "I've really not talked about my suspicions with anyone. Their leader, their Uncle George? He gave us the very briefest of overviews for why they are here, and his explanation was credible—as far as he went. But he really gave no indication of the exact nature of his objective, or even how he planned to carry it out."

Xander shook his head. "In other words, we've got no idea what he's really doing. Is he Mr. Rogers or Snidely Whiplash?"

"Exactly." Giles studied both Xander and Oz for a moment. "You said you talked to the three young men for quite a while. Did they give any indication of their uncle's plans?"

"They were pretty vague," Xander admitted.

Oz added, "My guess is that even they really don't know."

"They just told us things about their life."

"You know. How much fun it was to be a Druid."

"Indeed," Giles replied dryly, "I imagine it's all sorts of fun."

"Well," Xander said, "you do get to wear neat robes."

A good point, Oz thought. "And you can pull flowers out of thin air and cause little lightning bolts to come out of the ends of your fingers."

Xander nodded. "It's a great way to burn up crumbled wads of paper."

"Yeah. Well, these were the demonstrations they gave us last night."

"I think, every time we tried to talk too much about why they were here, they started demonstrating."

Oz thought there was more to it than that. "But there could be other reasons for what they did. You know, their father died the last time they tried to do this thing, whatever it is. It might be painful for them to talk about it."

"I guess the only thing we can do now is proceed with caution," Giles replied. "These Druids may indeed prove to be very helpful."

Xander grinned. "Is it all right if we let them teach us a few secrets?"

"I don't see what harm it can do, so long as the two of you watch out for each other, and you each keep an open mind. It would be wonderful if they were really what they said they were. Perhaps, with the Hellmouth out of commission, the Slayer, and her Watcher, too, could have a bit of a breather."

Wow. This whole Slayer/Hellmouth thing affected everybody. Oz had never thought about the toll it took on Giles as well.

"I've actually done some further research," Giles continued, "and found something very troubling. However, it may end up being reassuring."

Xander stared at the librarian. "Once more, with clarity?"

"I believe," Giles went on, "that after they were driven underground, the Druids fragmented. While some followed the ritual of nature worship, others were jealous of their loss of power and started to experiment with those darker forces which earlier they had only attempted to control. In fact, these offshoots of the Druids might even be responsible for some of the same calamities that our current group claims they must fix."

"So you think these guys want to bring about trouble rather than cure it?" Xander asked.

"Not exactly. But I fear they might want to try and control that dark side, an ambition that—we know from our own experience—could have no good end."

Giles threw up his hands. "Or my suspicions could be totally unfounded. We simply don't have enough information."

"Then information you will get!" Xander exclaimed. "This looks like a job for Xanderman. Quick, Oz! To the Xandermobile!"

Oz guessed that was as good an exit line as any.

* * *

Xander found Cordelia standing in the middle of the hallway. School had ended fifteen minutes ago, and the place was pretty empty. Except for Cordelia, who was busy staring into space.

"Hey, Cordy!" he called. "Funny meeting you here, out in the open like this. You know, without the comfy confines of a broom closet—"

He stopped. Cordelia was still staring.

"Hello!" Xander called. "Earth to Cordy!"

"Bryce," Cordelia replied.

"What?"

"Bryce Abbot."

"What? You mean the football player you used to go out with? The one who went away to college? It was a good thing you broke up with him. The man had no neck." Xander realized he was babbling. What was she thinking about an old boyfriend for? Was this why she was acting so strange lately?

Cordelia blinked. "Oh, Xander. I didn't hear—my mind—" She frowned. "I've got a million problems with the dance."

Again with the dance. Maybe she wanted to go with Bryce Abbot rather than Xander. Well, he didn't have to stand around and take this.

"Well, don't let me get in the way of the mambo," Xander said. "I've got to go out and help some Druids."

"You do?" Cordelia was still frowning. "Well, I guess I've got a lot to do, too."

Well, if she was going to treat him like that, he

could treat her like that, too. "See ya," he said, and turned to go.

He walked quickly down the hall. As he turned the corner, he thought he heard Cordy call his name. Nah. It was probably his imagination. Or she wanted to ask him some dumb question about his tux.

Keep on walking, Xander, my boy.

It was time for some Druid action.

Buffy saw the big black car screech to a halt in front of the high school. Ian's brother Tom waved from the driver's seat. Xander and Oz rushed right past Buffy without a word, quickly jumping down the steps to the car.

"Okay!" Xander called. "Time to learn the secrets of the ancients!"

"Time for Tom to learn to drive on the right side of the road!" Dave's voice called from somewhere inside the huge Caddy.

"Actually," Tom said. "It's mostly time to run some errands. I think our uncle's too busy to talk to you today. But maybe we can show you a couple of card tricks."

Xander and Oz piled into the back seat and the car tore away.

Nobody had paid the slightest attention to Buffy. *And why should they?* She hadn't even heard Ian's voice. He probably wasn't even in the car. *And why should I care about it anyway?*

It hurt so much when she lost Angel. He was back,

but they both agreed she needed to look elsewhere. Loving Angel was too dangerous.

She needed to get moving, make a statement. But the vampires wouldn't be out for another few hours. And she had promised her mother she wouldn't burn down another school.

She wondered if she still had that junk food back in her locker.

Chapter 13

IAN ENTERED THE ROOM WHERE HIS UNCLE WAS WAITing. He could see why the people from Sunnydale would be suspicious. As he got closer to what he had to do, Uncle George seemed to grow more tight-lipped. Now, unless Ian or his brothers dragged it out of him, he wasn't even explaining things to his nephews.

Uncle George glanced up at Ian for only an instant, then went back to looking into the divining crystal he had brought, as though, if he just looked long enough, the crystal would hold all the answers. The crystal was a small, multifaceted stone, translucent with a hint of blue. Whenever Ian had seen it, it struck him as looking very cold.

Ian waited a moment to see if his uncle would acknowledge his presence. For their stay in Sunnydale, they had rented what had been advertised as a "furnished cottage" on the edge of town, but it was unlike any cottage Ian had seen before. It resembled nothing so much as the semidetached suburban homes around Cardiff, a boxy structure with white walls and shag carpet. The furnishings all seemed to be twenty years old, a mismatched set of plaid couches and overstuffed chairs which wouldn't have looked out of place in a seventies American sitcom. It was the least natural home Ian had ever seen, and the last place you would think to find a Druid, which Ian guessed suited Uncle George just fine. Still, it was quiet out here. Their neighbors all appeared to be software engineers who were never home. *Ideal,* he supposed, *if you were working on a spell to save the world. . . .*

Ian decided he'd had enough of his uncle and his crystal. "You've sent Dave and Tom into town," Ian said. "But you said you need me here. Why?"

His uncle frowned without looking away from the stone. "It is time to begin. And it is time for you to accept responsibility."

Ian thought he heard a hint of accusation in his uncle's voice. "I have always been willing to share my part of the load. Especially now. You know how important this is to all of us—especially after the death of my father."

"I do not want to speak of your father,'" his uncle replied without emotion. "I want to speak about what is happening now."

Ian winced. The death of his father, George's brother, had affected them all. All of them felt responsible, but his Uncle George seemed to be taking it hardest of all. He wouldn't talk about what had happened, but he was driven to change it.

Ian peered over his uncle's shoulder, trying to get a better view of the smoky blue gem stone on the table before them. He was not as adept at reading the crystal as his elders, but even he could see images flickering in the stone, images clearer than any he had seen before, due, no doubt, to the power of the Hellmouth. But what were these images? Green. For *nature?* Red stones. Blood? Aids to their uncle's upcoming incantation? Or predictions of what would come if they triumphed—or failed?

"And what is happening now?" Ian demanded. "You don't seem to want to tell anybody, even your own nephews."

"Nonsense. We are among strangers. I simply do not wish to reveal too much—"

"But weren't you the one who told me that we very well may need the strangers, especially the Slayer, if we hope to succeed?"

George finally turned to look at his nephew. "I did. So much seems to change from minute to minute. Conditions are different here. We are so far from home. But the Slayer and her friends—do you think we can get their help?"

"Well, they have their suspicions."

George shook his head. "Considering the way we arrived, that is only natural."

Ian was glad his uncle at least realized that. He

added, "But I think if we are as open as we can be, they will join us."

"I hope so." George gestured at the crystal before him. "There are treacherous turns to the course we take. There are those who are pledged to stop us. It will help us greatly if we can bring the Slayer in to protect us while we finish our task."

"So you need—the Slayer." Ian had a little trouble even saying her name. He swallowed. He couldn't let his personal feelings interfere with what had to be done. "You've told me this before, but you've never explained exactly why."

His uncle shook his head. "This place of power—the Hellmouth—is so much greater than those I have dealt with in the past. I suppose it makes me nervous. I may have to make adjustments to the spells in order to succeed. And what if I err, and some of that which we are meant to stop breaks free?"

"So we bring in the Slayer. But if we have such an accident, won't it be dangerous?"

"If we have such an accident, and the Slayer cannot stop it, it will kill us all."

And probably mean the end of the world, Ian thought. That was why the Druids were here, why they had thrown aside two thousand years of secrecy to reveal themselves, not only here, but all over the world.

"And what of the others?"

"The other groups, at the other great points?" George shook his head again. "Perhaps, if one of us fails, the others can still find ways to slow the destructive forces. Or perhaps a single error will destroy every one of us."

Ian was finding this conversation frustrating. He found every conversation with his uncle frustrating. "We're really only feeding the people here small pieces of the puzzle. Why don't we tell the Watcher and the Slayer of the enormity of our undertaking? Surely that will convince them to help us."

"Would it? I don't know. There are still so many changes we may have to make."

"Changes?" Ian didn't like the sound of this. "But I thought the elders agreed. We were going to repeat the spell my father devised—"

George made a shooing motion with his hands, as if waving away his nephew's objections. "No doubt we will, but perhaps with some minor modifications. The elders are half a world away. They do not even know of the subtle changes I already see around me."

George was speaking in riddles again. What wasn't his uncle talking about? Ian was afraid he knew.

"You are going to . . . to try the other spell, aren't you?"

George looked away. "I will try whatever is needed. You know how desperate the situation might be."

"So you say."

"So your father said," George insisted. "Look, I will show you as much of this as possible, get you to see the truth, in case the same thing happens to me that happened to your father."

And the spell will consume you the same way it consumed my father. Ian repressed a shudder.

"Uncle, I hope not."

His uncle let the slightest of smiles crease his face. "Not half so much as I do. But this must be done."

Perhaps, Ian thought, *I'm being too critical.* His uncle had a lifetime of training. He knew the dangers and what must be done to overcome them.

"As you say," Ian replied at last. "But about the Slayer and her friends? They know in their hearts what is happening here—and I believe it is that knowledge that will cause them to side with us."

But his uncle was adamant. "We can't get too close to any of them. We may work with them, but each side will always have their secrets."

Surely, Ian thought, his uncle had his reasons. And Ian knew he had reasons of his own. He found it difficult—impossible, really, to think unemotionally about anything that had to do with that young Vampire Slayer. Her image filled his mind. The way her blond hair moved in the moonlight. The strength she showed against adversity. The way her lips curled when she smiled.

He had never been attracted to a girl in the same way as the Slayer. The more his uncle insisted on distance, the more he thought about Buffy.

Maybe a single night. What difference did it make if the world was going to end anyway?

"Ian?" His uncle's voice broke his reverie. "We must begin."

Ian sighed. He had no time for flights of fancy. He should think of nothing but the work.

His uncle held a piece of paper in his hand. "I will need the following."

His uncle had made out a list. Ian had no idea where to get most of these things in California. Perhaps he could ask Xander and Oz to help.

Even at first glance, Ian could tell that the list was far too long. Only about half of the items listed were a part of his father's second spell. The rest of them—

"I recognize this plan. This is the spell that killed my father. The elders agreed that we would not follow this path again."

"The elders are not here! We will have a very short time to right the way. I plan to prepare both spells. I will use the other first. If that does not succeed—well, I pray that I have made better preparations against attack than the last time."

Ian did not feel good about this. His uncle was even keeping secrets from his family and the elders.

There were too many secrets here.

His uncle seemed to read his mind. "You must trust me on this. Your brothers will return shortly. The three of you will work together to prepare the spell the elders have chosen."

So Ian would gather the items on the list. "And in the meantime, what will you do?"

"I will spend every minute determining if there is a way to employ the other spell in safety. Your father made too many compromises. I feel we must return to the true ancient teachings."

Ian didn't like the sound of that. "The true ancient teachings? There are practices in there which we abandoned hundreds of years ago."

"Perhaps that was wrong. The Druids have employed great power over the years. Perhaps we must return to that." His uncle paused, looking straight in Ian's eyes. "I realize in so doing, I might destroy the order. But even that might be worth it, if I can save the world."

As sincere as his uncle seemed, Ian still had his doubts.

"Yet, this decision—"

"It is not your decision to make." His uncle cut him off. He turned back to the crystal before him. "I will be in contact with the others."

So his uncle had ended the discussion, and Ian was bound to obey his elder. He knew it was his destiny. Dare he draw the Slayer in as well?

He knew that was up to fate.

Sunnydale had seemed, for the last couple of days, like a haven from the cares of the world. Even the fights with the vampires had felt more like sport than a matter of life or death. Ian realized that was because the Slayer was there. In some imaginary world that could never be, he and the Slayer might always fight side by side.

How could that imaginary world ever come to be?

The very thought of Buffy made sweat break out on his palms. He knew he had been avoiding her. Once or twice, he had been outright rude.

But he wasn't here to improve his social life. He, his brothers, his uncle—they were trying to prevent evil from overwhelming the world.

Ian knew he would have to tell her of his feelings.

His mind returned to this, over and over again.

A Druid's life was hard, his education, taxing. He hadn't had much time for romance—a pair of flings a year or two ago—but since the crisis began, he hadn't had time for anything.

Perhaps he and the Slayer could have a moment together.

For one who followed his path, that would have to be enough.

Well, here Gloria was, back in the alley again—another night, another master plan. Cordelia had gone back into her little club. *Gloria's supposed to watch little Cordelia, Naomi says. But the Slayer's in that club, too. Gloria saw her go in. The Slayer could recognize Gloria. Then where would Gloria be? She'd be staked in the heart, turned into a pile of dust. What good would Gloria be as a pile of dust? No good at all!*

Naomi was gone too. Gloria liked it better when Naomi was gone, when Gloria could think for herself. She'd follow Cordelia home when she left the Bronze. But that wouldn't be for hours.

Gloria heard a noise from the other side of the alley, and remembered she wasn't completely alone.

"Bryce," she called. "Naomi's gone. It's safe to come out."

Naomi could freeze Cordelia with some spell, and it looked like she kept Bryce frozen with fear. But Gloria? Gloria was already a vampire. What else could go wrong?

"Bryce?" Gloria called. "I think we need to get to know each other better."

She heard a rustling among the garbage bags.

"That's it, Bryce. You have to get out of your hiding place more often. Actually, what's life worth without a little companionship?" She giggled. "Heck. I'm already dead, and I need companionship, too!"

The thing that was once a quarterback shuffled out into the open.

"What a nice Bryce! Poor boy, Naomi's done such nasty things to you—you being a star quarterback and all. I bet you have some real muscles under all that grime."

The Bryce thing moaned.

"Hey, we got to stick together. Otherwise, Naomi will drive us crazy."

The Bryce thing growled.

Gloria smiled and strolled toward the creature. "What Naomi doesn't know won't hurt her, at least not yet. There are a lot of lonely nights in Sunnydale." She giggled. "You want a little vampire love?"

She gently pushed back the matted hair from his

forehead. There were a pair of eyes in there somewhere.

This was the first time she'd ever done anything with anyone even resembling a quarterback. *Take that, Naomi,* she thought.

Hey, vampires couldn't be choosers.

Chapter 14

BUFFY HAD RARELY SEEN SUNNYDALE SO QUIET. IF IT was slow the night before, tonight it was dead—no pun intended. No people, no vampires, no cars, no dogs. She was all alone out here. It was like this place had become Sleepy Hollow or something.

And the quieter it got, the more she thought about Ian. Why? He wouldn't even speak to her. But the way he looked at her and the way he got flustered when she was near—she knew those signs. She guessed she wasn't as out of practice in the dating game as she thought.

She liked the way he handled himself in a fight, too. As the Slayer, she spent too much time working on her own moves. It was nice to check out somebody else's for a change.

She also liked the way he'd shown up—twice now—just in the nick of time. She started wishing something would happen so Ian could show up again.

Whoa, slow down! What are you thinking about? Girl, you've got too much free time on your hands.

Buffy jumped.

It was only a flock of birds, just down the street, over in the graveyard. But any sound would have been startling after all that silence, and the birds were making a tremendous racket.

Well, Buffy thought, *if anything is going to happen, it would happen in the graveyard.* As far as the Slayer was concerned, it was Sunnydale's action hot spot.

Buffy walked, quickly but carefully, over to the cemetery gate, on the lookout for the usual pale faces. Vampires loved the graveyard. It was their home—at least for a lot of them. Even the Master used to live nearby, though not by choice, right above the Hellmouth.

The Hellmouth. Buffy wondered if whatever was going on with the birds had something to do with the Druids' spell. She certainly didn't see any vampires. Not a single one. Which, she realized, also might have come from the Druids' spell. That was probably one of the advantages of being so secretive. People would give you credit for just about anything.

She stepped through the gate and walked across the well-manicured grass of the all-too-familiar cemetery. She moved slowly toward the noisy birds, ready for attack. Did she catch some movement between the graves? Was it the Druids performing some ritual? Or were the dead coming back to life—like usual?

She walked over to take a closer look.

Hello. Things waved just above the ground, but they didn't look human, living or dead. They almost looked like tentacles. Buffy moved forward more slowly and saw the tentacles were sprouting leaves. They were vines, or branches—vegetation of some sort—growing as she watched, a foot or more every minute. The growing vines made a soft shooshing sound as the leaves rubbed against the ground, the gravestones, and other growing vines. The softer noise had been lost under the racket of the birds, but now most of the flock was flying off, looking, no doubt, for a calmer part of town. Buffy wondered if she should do the same thing.

This had to be some part of the Druids' spell. Giles had mentioned they were big on nature. Maybe they would surround the Hellmouth with a wall of nature. The vines curled around the gravestones and monuments, twisted around the shrubs and trees. Yes, this sudden growth must be some sort of barrier, some preparation for the greater spell to come.

Buffy felt the ground move beneath her feet. Small shoots were poking their way through the soil all around her, new tendrils of the massive plant that would take over the cemetery. But she was here by herself; there was no one else in danger, no need for the Slayer. She should let the spell run its course, then ask the Druids—ask Ian—what it was really all about.

The vampires would be somewhere else tonight. It was time to go—

Her feet stuck to the ground. She couldn't lift her boots. She looked down and saw a web of dark green covering the leather. The tendrils had already curled over both of her shoes and were anchoring her feet firmly to the soil.

She tried jerking her feet free, but the tiny network of vines held her ankles tight. She was trapped here. In the middle of the graveyard, the vines were covering everything, turning grave markers green, draping leafy boas over marble angels, swallowing trees and bushes whole. In a moment, the vines would cover her as well.

She shouldn't panic. She was the Slayer. She had been in much worse places than this. She had defeated bunches of vampires, monsters, and demons by the truckload. She wouldn't let some overactive poison ivy do her in.

Her feet were caught, but for now, these tendrils were very close to the ground. She knelt down and quickly unzipped her boots. New shoots tickled her hands, tried to wrap themselves around her fingers. She jerked her hands free, breaking a couple of the more delicate shoots, and pulled her feet free of the boots, then ran from the center of the spell. New growth popped up all around her, almost tripping her twice. She vaulted over a low gravestone. If she were to fall now, she might never get free.

She stopped at last when she reached the asphalt. Nothing grew through the blacktop; it was smooth and cool beneath her sock-clad feet. The spell seemed to be centered on the lawn behind her. She turned back to look at it and saw that what was once a cemetery was now becoming a jungle.

This had to be a part of the Druids' spell. But why hadn't they told her about it—warned her about it? Luckily no one else was out here tonight. She might have been trapped and squeezed to death or smothered. These plants were serious business.

She planned to give the Druids—she planned to give Ian—a piece of her mind.

At last, Cordelia thought. She and Xander had some private time.

They had found a quiet back corner of the Bronze and were doing some big-time smooching. Cordelia didn't realize how much she had missed this until she was nestled back in Xander's arms. She closed her eyes and listened to the band as she felt Xander's warmth, smelled his good, clean smell, kissed his sweet lips.

What's that? She started, mid-kiss. She thought she heard a voice. What had it said?

There was nothing now. The rock band wailed on. No, she must have only heard the singer.

"You comfortable?" Xander whispered.

"Um-hmm," she replied.

"Me too," Xander said. "We've got to do this more often."

On that, Cordelia thought, *the two of us are in complete agree—*

There it was again! That voice. Not the singer—no, something higher, fainter—maybe a backup voice. What was it saying?

It was calling her name.

Oh . . .

Cordelia pulled away.

"Listen, Xander. I've got to—"

"What?" he asked.

She frowned. She didn't want to be anywhere but right here, right now.

The voice again. The insistent voice.

She wriggled away. "No, I really have to—"

"What?" Xander grinned at her. "I don't mind. As long as you come back."

"Come back? Yes, come back."

She pushed herself away from him and ran quickly across the room, pushing her way past the crowd, running into dancers. Nothing mattered.

Nothing but where I have to be. . . .

Was it something he said?

One minute, everything was forgotten. He'd come back from his afternoon with the Druids and Cordelia hadn't said the words "Bryce Abbott" once. Xander and Cordelia were in make out heaven.

The next, she acted like she had to go put out a fire. Actually, she ran away fast enough to put out three or four fires.

Maybe it was his breath. No. They'd been kissing

so long that by now they'd performed a complete saliva transfusion. His breath was her breath. End of story.

Maybe it was those burgers they'd eaten earlier. Maybe he'd suddenly developed a zit that looked like a second nose. Xander sighed. Maybe, like, it could be anything.

Could she be going to see Bryce? What was he—just some college-age star-quarterback ex-boyfriend of Cordy's? What could she see in Bryce that she couldn't she in Xander? What *couldn't* she see?

It was that expression on her face as she ran that bothered him. Well, that and the fact that she ran away from him in the first place. If she had given him a little smile and said "Back in a minute!" he would have just sat here, Mr. Happy Guy, while she powdered her nose or got a drink of water or talked to Amanda about some detail of the formal dance that just couldn't wait—whatever. But in that second before she left—Xander thought he'd never seen Cordelia look quite so frantic, ever.

Maybe it took until this minute for her to realize her horrible mistake. Maybe she opened her eyes and said "I'm kissing Xander Harris?"

Let's face it, Xander thought. He wasn't the formal-dance type. Maybe Cordelia realized she could find someone her own speed somewhere else.

Someone like Bryce.

What if she had realized it weeks ago and was already seeing somebody else? What if she was just looking to let him down easy? Maybe all her disappearances had nothing to do with the Spring Formal and everything to do with some guy on the football team—on the local *college* football team!

Wow, Xander certainly hoped not. Maybe she just had an upset stomach. Not that he'd wish an upset stomach on her, but compared to breaking up—well, stomachs came and went. Relationships were serious.

Where'd she go? Xander had been startled; she disappeared before he could do anything. And now he couldn't do anything but keep time with the band and hope she'd come back.

Five minutes passed, then ten. This was just too strange. Next time this happened, Xander decided, he would definitely follow her.

Cordelia didn't like this at all. One moment, she was finally snuggling with Xander, the next, she was all alone, and in the alley besides.

"It's time for my dinner."

Cordelia blinked. The whole Naomi business came back to her. The threats . . . the fear . . . the cold.

Oh, no. She wasn't going to be treated this way by anybody—even if it was a vampire. She tried to turn up her nose, but her face was frozen again.

"Get stuffed!" she said instead.

Naomi's face floated before her own. "Dear Cordelia. You still don't realize that you have no choice.

It should be obvious that I can bring you to me whenever I want. And soon it will be clear that I can make you *do* whatever I want, too."

Naomi laughed quietly. "Now you'll bring me dinner. Don't worry. It won't be anybody close to you the first time. I want this more like a practice run."

Cordelia couldn't move. And Naomi was right. Cordelia had felt compelled to leave Xander and come out here, going from one of the best moments in her life to one of the worst. And now Cordelia was supposed to go back into the Bronze and come out with someone for Naomi to kill?

She wouldn't do it. She couldn't do it!

Cordelia had to think of a way out of this. Only questions came to mind. How could she stop Naomi—how could she stop doing things for Naomi—when most of the time she couldn't even remember the vampire was here?

Cordelia was becoming very afraid.

She felt the vampire's cold whisper in her ear:

"Now Cordelia! Do it now!"

Cordelia blinked. Here she was again, out in the alley behind the Bronze. Boy, she must really like it out here. The fresh air, maybe? The privacy—a place to get away from the crowds? Or maybe close, personal contact with all this garbage?

Cordelia wrinkled her nose. She didn't think so. Why would she want to get away from Xander? But she couldn't think of Xander just now.

There was something she had to do inside the Bronze.

There she is!

Xander felt a great rush of relief when he saw Cordelia talking to the other girl by the back door. It was only after he realized she was safe that he got annoyed. She had said she'd come right back. Why was she standing around at the other end of the Bronze talking to some perfect stranger?

Well, just because he didn't know the girl didn't mean Cordelia didn't know her. The other girl looked to be about their age; probably even went to their high school. Until very recently, he had to remind himself, he and Cordelia moved in different circles—maybe different dimensions.

Well, right now their circles were going to get a lot closer. He walked over to the two girls.

"Isn't it a little stuffy in here?" Cordelia was saying.

"Hi!" Xander called as he approached.

Cordelia gave him the briefest of glances. She looked very confused. "Oh—uh, hi Xander. I'll talk to you later."

Xander wasn't going to be brushed off that easily. He decided he'd hang around and wait for a good place to break into the conversation.

"So," Cordelia continued, ignoring Xander completely, "I saw you talking with that new guy."

"Dave?" the girl asked.

"Yeah, he's one of Amanda's cousins. Foreign guys are so cute. Can you dig those accents?"

Wait a minute, Xander thought. *Is this the same Cordelia?* The last time he'd talked with her about the three Druids, she had pronounced them the most boring people on the face of the planet!

"Hey, Cordelia." He tried to break in again. "I was thinking, maybe I could actually talk to the girl I came to the Bronze to see—"

"No Xander," she replied, not even looking at him. "Go and sit down."

What? That was it? No explanation, no apology, just "go and sit down?"

For once in his life, Xander was speechless.

Cordelia, apparently, wanted to talk enough for both of them. She pressed on with the other girl. "It's a little crowded in here for what I've got to tell you. Why don't we go outside?"

"Outside?" the other woman asked incredulously.

"Well, yeah," Cordelia said with a knowing smirk. "Listen, Barb. There's a back stairway here that nobody ever watches."

There is? Xander tried to think about what Cordelia was talking about. Well, there was that fire exit that led to that back alley out by the Dumpster—not exactly the place for romance, and the last place he'd expect to see Cordelia.

"Really?" Barb asked.

"Yeah. When you're still stuck living at home, you have to find those special private places for—you know. Barb, trust me. I know my way around."

This was definitely something Xander did not want to hear.

But Barb was half-way sold. "Well, if what you're going to tell me is really juicy—"

Cordelia shook her head. "Listen. What I heard Marti say to Anton about your old boyfriend, Bill—but no. I have to tell you in private. She smiled conspiratorially. "People do talk, you know."

Barb made a face. "Who pays attention to anybody in here? Everybody's already busy with somebody or they're off listening to the music."

It didn't make any sense to Xander, either. What was Cordelia trying to pull? Was this some kind of practical joke?

"Listen, I'm not worried. I just don't want this juicy dish to get around. And afterward, we'll go over and talk to Dave. Dave!" she called, waving at Amanda's cousin, who had just walked in on the other side of the room. "See you later!"

Dave smiled and waved back. He began to push his way through the throng.

"Oh," Barb said brightly. "Here comes Dave now."

Cordelia tugged at her arm. "Don't you want to hear the secret? Trust me, you'll just about die."

Xander stepped in their way. "Cordy, when you get back, I want to . . ."

"Xander?" Cordelia blinked. "Well, okay. I just—just—" She frowned as if she couldn't get out the words. She turned and reached for him. "Xander! I need—I need—"

What was the matter? Cordelia looked like she was going to faint.

Xander stepped forward as Cordelia shook her head. "No, I'm fine now." She glared at Xander. "Didn't I tell you to leave me alone?"

Xander took a step away. Cordelia had her share of wiggy moments—everybody did, Xander supposed. But right now she was throwing a Dolly Parton special. This last little while that he and Cordelia had been together, he'd thought he'd gotten to know her pretty well, but this Cordelia Chase seemed like a complete stranger.

"Come on, Barb." Cordy grabbed the other girl's elbow. "These men can wait."

Dave caught up with Xander as the girls hurried away.

"Hey!" Dave said. "Didn't they want to talk to me?"

"That Alex, is the Final Jeopardy question," Xander agreed. "Who knows what they're doing. But I'm going to find out."

Xander pushed his way through the crowd. He noticed that Dave was right behind him. He had to figure what was going on here. This was no longer weird. It felt to Xander like something far worse.

He caught up to them at the back stairway. It was indeed the fire exit, the one with the sign that said Opening This Door Will Cause Alarm to Sound! Except, Xander noticed, the door was already open.

Barb was already halfway up the stairs. Dave

looked from Cordelia to Barb and back again, probably not wanting to be rude, but probably wanting Cordelia to go away so he could spend some quality time with the other girl.

Well, Xander thought, *time for me to do my part for romantic relationships.* If he and Cordelia were on the skids, maybe he could at least give Dave and Barb some privacy.

"Hey, Cordelia!" he called as he trotted toward the fire exit.

"Xander!" Her eyes rolled. "I told I thought you to get—I thought I told you—I can't help—I don't want—get away from me, now! It's not safe! It's—I never want to see you again!"

Dave smiled apologetically. "Well, I guess I'll let you two work this out." He ran up the stairs and out the door that Barb had disappeared through only a moment before.

This time, Cordelia did faint. Xander caught her before she could fall. He held her there for a minute, watching lines of tension leave her face. She looked like a sleeping child.

She opened her eyes. "Xander?"

"Cordelia?"

She turned her head to look at her surroundings. "What are we doing back here?"

"You were the one who came back here, you and Barb."

"Barb?" Cordelia looked confused. "From junior high school? I haven't talked to her in years."

What? Didn't she remember anything?

"Cordelia, something's going on here. Some spell kind of thing."

"What do you mean?"

That's when the racket started.

Naomi recognized the first victim as she walked into the alley. Barb was her name, a minor hanger-on in their old crowd. The sort of person people would barely miss.

Cordelia had done her job well.

"Barb!" she called.

Barb turned at the sound of her voice. "Naomi? I haven't seen you in ages!" She looked around the alley, sniffed at the pungent aroma of the garbage across the way.

"Ewww," she said, wrinkling her nose. "There's a reason this place is private."

"Oh," Naomi replied. "This alley isn't anywhere near as bad as you think. For some of us, it can be quite exciting."

"Exciting?" Barb glanced back at the door to the Bronze. "I'm waiting for Cordy to join me. Are you waiting for somebody?"

"Somebody?" Naomi glided toward the young woman. "No, I just want to talk to you, Barb. I've always felt the two of us should be much closer."

"Closer?" Barb looked down at the point where Naomi grabbed her arm. "Ewww! Your hand is like ice!" Naomi used her other hand to grab Barb's shoulder and draw her near.

"What are you doing?" Barb shouted. She wriggled and squirmed. Her strength was no match for that of a vampire. "No!"

"Yes," Naomi whispered.

Barb's struggles ended as soon as Naomi's fangs entered her neck.

Ah. It feels so good to sink your teeth into tender young flesh. Now, she would drink deep and let the warmth replenish her.

"Hey!"

Naomi opened her eyes. Some young man stood before her. Cordelia was working overtime. Very well. She would drain Barb and take him next.

Naomi felt herself jerked away from her meal. The young man had landed a flying kick in her ribs.

"Barb!" he called. "Get behind me!"

"Dave?" the young woman murmured, already drowsy from the loss of blood.

Naomi roared in frustration. No one interrupted her feeding! She would grab this puny human male and rip him in half, then lap his blood up from the street! Then, she would finish the girl—a meal and dessert.

She rushed forward to seize the boy, but he was no longer there. Another kick to her back sent her reeling forward into the piled garbage.

"Come on, Barb!" Naomi heard behind her. "We'll get you out of here. We'll get help."

No, they wouldn't. Humans might surprise her once, might even get lucky, twice. But she was a vampire. Vampires prevailed.

She tried to calm her blood lust. Sheer animal ferocity might not be the easiest way to end this. The boy was obviously a trained fighter. But Naomi was faster. If she could study his moves for a moment, she would discover his weaknesses. Draining him then would be even more satisfying!

She rose from among the garbage bags and brushed off her gown. "You're not going anywhere, Dave. This is your and Barb's last date—ever."

She approached him more warily this time. If she could get the boy in her grip, get her fangs in his neck, she would win. It was merely a matter of anticipating his next move. Then, it would be time to feast!

She reached out her right hand. He shifted slightly to his left. She took a step away. He rested lightly on the balls of his feet as if he wasn't scared of her in the least. That would be his undoing.

"Barb?" he called over his shoulder. "Are you all right?"

"Dave?" Barb's voice weakly answered. "I think so. What happened?"

"I'll explain later. Do you see any bits of wood in the alley? Anything with a sharp edge?"

So this boy knew what she was and how to destroy her. Perhaps, Naomi thought, she had been too full of herself. Perhaps she could use a little assistance to rid herself of this pest.

"Bryce!" she called. "Where are you? I need you!"

But there was no sound from among the garbage

bags, no noise save the breathing and the heartbeats of the two humans before her.

"Bryce!" she called. "Gloria!"

There was nothing. Naomi was alone.

This wasn't supposed to happen. Her servants were supposed to be there for her.

The boy took a step toward her. Could he sense her fear? She was stronger than he was! She could destroy him in an instant.

The boy smiled. There was a sharpened piece of wood in his hand.

It won't happen like this!

Naomi took a step away.

"I'll destroy you all!" she cried.

And then she ran.

Chapter 15

GEORGE COULD NOT STOP LOOKING AT THE CRYSTAL. No doubt when his nephew had been in the room, Ian had thought he was using the gem to try to foretell the future. But all he could see in the facets before him was his past.

Deep in the stone, over and over again, it showed him what had happened before.

No! Don't let them nearer! Don't let them!

George closed his eyes. For years, the elders had foretold of a great danger. And the forces of darkness did appear to be shifting, the supernatural gaining power. George and his brother Stephen had seen the signs. They knew the teachings, they knew how the teachings had changed. Together, they volunteered to defeat the evil that was to come.

The two of them had gathered the likely spells, checked the portents to determine the most auspicious date, and figured what they thought to be the safest course to dispel the growing danger to the world. At last it had come down to the choice between two different spells. They argued for weeks over the best path to take: a spell of light and crystal, which would seal the dark forces away, much, George guessed, as the great vampire called the Master had been trapped beneath these very streets; or a darker, older spell, which would send the dark things reeling back into those places from which they first came. The second spell was the more decisive of the two, but that second spell called for blood.

Stephen had been the talented one, the one with the true facility for magic. George was more the scholar, his own spells often halting and clumsy. He would succeed more often than not, but even he admitted that his conjurings spent more time going around the barn than entering through the front door.

Stephen was the one who would oversee the spell, so Stephen's judgment won out in the end. They would use the magic derived from light rather than blood and attempt to entrap those forces that would do them harm. Once bound, the elders might find a way at their leisure to banish these things forever. It had seemed so logical at the time.

No! Don't let them nearer! Don't let them!

So, on the vernal equinox nearly a year ago, they had begun. Neither one of them had known it would be so hard.

Only after the spell had begun did they realize they had made a bad choice of location. The ancient point of power was weak, the connection with the darker things far too tenuous. Still Stephen plowed forward, trying to ensnare the dark forces in his web of light.

And Stephen had managed to strengthen the connection, but by doing so he forged a link that allowed the dark things—the ten thousand demons of legend—to enter the mortal, material world and destroy the spellcaster.

No! Don't let them nearer! Don't let them!

George! George!

There were three levels of Stephen's spell. First, a connection, second, a strengthening, and third, the seal through which the dark forces could not penetrate. George and Stephen's three sons had assisted Stephen's plans, weaving secondary spells of strength and protection, and all had gone well, until the great white light Stephen had produced changed, deepening from yellow to orange to darkest red.

"What should I do?" George called. The light surrounded them, so strong it was almost blinding. George could barely see his brother, only a few feet away. His nephews, perhaps a score of paces distant, were totally lost to view.

"Hurry!" Stephen had called. "Begin the third part of the spell!"

And then the light had brought the others. Stephen panicked.

"They're all over me! No! No! Don't let them nearer! Don't let them! George! George!"

George had to do something. The first spell would not work. He knew the other, darker spell by heart. He had made all the preparations in case they might be needed. He would push the demons back. He would banish them forever!

He needed blood. In the last desperate moment, he opened his own veins.

But as he made the cut, Stephen seemed to break free of the things.

"No!" his brother called. "I can turn them back! I can complete the spell! George! What are you—"

It was too late. George's spell had already been set in motion.

The two spells together seemed to create a moment of vacuum, a moment when the things might reach out a final time.

The red light was gone, but Stephen was surrounded by flame. He scream lasted only an instant. In an instant, he was consumed.

The spells righted themselves. Something in the combination had worked. The dark things had been banished, at least for a time. But all that was left of Stephen was a charred corpse.

And all that was left to George was his brother's final scream.

The blood—George's blood—was not enough.

The demons were repelled. But not before they had killed Stephen and left George to relive the moment over and over again.

The scream—his brother's final agony, seemed to reverberate from the stone. It hid the future. It hid the signs. It hid everything.

George had wanted to save them all. He never imagined the second spell would lead to his brother's death.

The three boys had been blinded by the spell. Only Stephen had seen George make the cuts. And Stephen was gone.

No one else had to know. George knew, and he would bear the burden until he took what the two brothers had tried to accomplish and succeeded at last. The responsibility, and the risk, would all be his. But he would succeed at any cost.

It had been nearly a year since his brother had lost his life, a year for George to master not one spell, but two, and he would use whichever of the two would ensure defeating the dark forces. He owed it to his brother, and to the world.

So he sent the boys to gather the necessary items, and to perform the preliminary incantations. Even now, Tom, the most talented of the three, was working on an incantation that would bind the Hellmouth in such a way that any demon seeking to pass through the gate would be destroyed. As the spell became more complex, Ian and Dave would join in. Then, tomorrow night, George would begin the final preparation.

There were other tasks that required his attention. But he could not pull his gaze from the stone. Why didn't the gem show him what was to come?

George looked up from the accusing crystal.

Someone—or something—else had entered the room.

He looked to the shadows.

"What are you doing here?"

The shadows took form—a tall man, with dark hair, an aristocratic nose, a cruel smile. *No,* George reminded himself. *Not a man.*

A vampire, who called himself Eric.

"You know you wanted to see me," Eric said.

George realized that he did. Eric was an emissary from the darkness. He had found George in Wales, after the accident. Somehow, he had found George again.

George was fascinated by this creature. By understanding him, he would come to know what he was to fight.

Eric chuckled. "I'm the only one who isn't frightened by you." He shook his head. "Most of my kind have left town. I've never seen such an exodus. Only the fools, or those too self-involved to see—only they stayed behind."

George was an elder in the oldest sect upon the face of the earth. He might be curious about this creature, he might even be able to use him, but he would not be intimidated.

"So which are you," he asked, "self-involved or a fool?"

Eric raised his right eyebrow in amusement. "I am neither, which is why you talk to me now. Only I realized there is no running away from you. Only I have followed you here to see this to the end. Your spell, while originating at the Hellmouth, will blanket the whole world."

"That is true," George admitted.

"It is amazing the wisdom you can gain from a few hundred years of existence," Eric replied calmly. "You should try it some time."

"My kind has passed wisdom down for thousands of years, and we will not rest until your kind is driven from the earth."

"Really? Then you aren't considering my earlier offer?" Eric's smile broadened to show a bit of teeth. "Everything I've told you so far is true. It's all a matter of survival. You guarantee mine, and I will guarantee yours."

"That sounded like a threat," George bristled. "I will not be stopped by the likes of you!"

"Georgie, Georgie, Georgie. You haven't been listening. I have no objection to your spell. The ancient magics will seal the Hellmouth for a hundred years. They will also guarantee the status quo for those who are prepared."

Eric stepped farther into the light. His eyes glowed red beneath the overhead bulb. "Think of it, George. There are certain changes that are too great. To cut all the supernatural off from the world might be as disastrous as allowing this evil to spawn. Your people's way is one of balance. You are a part of that balance, and so am I.

"There is something in this very town that proves

my point. What is the Slayer if there are no vampires? Pretty boring, let me tell you. Leave a little mystery in the world. She'll thank you for it."

"So you are doing this to benefit the Slayer?"

"You know why I do this." The vampire spread his arms wide. "This is my moment," Eric crowed. "There were always those above me. I knew there would be a time when I would rise to the top."

Perhaps, George thought, *the same might be true for me.*

With a sudden clarity, he realized how much he wished for that—all the other elders humbled, realizing at last that only *he* was right.

"There will be benefits for both of us," Eric continued. "An alliance between us will allow you to control the Hellmouth for a hundred years, destroying anything that might pass and anything that might challenge me for mastery of the night. I only wish to survive, and perhaps to prosper a bit. Even though the evil will be contained, the power will remain, a power that will sustain me, and I will be king in this small domain.

"Perhaps the Slayer will kill me then. All I ask is a chance. And to get that chance, I must make sure that you succeed. The Slayer might have helped you fight back the forces of darkness. But I can attack them from the inside, subvert them, protect you completely."

George was surprised. Before, Eric had only spoken of knowledge. This was a new offer. "Protection? I will have to think about it."

Eric nodded. "You and I know it is almost time. Answer me tomorrow."

The vampire faded back into the shadows.

George stood, but there was no longer any sign of the creature.

There were too many questions here and no time to find answers. George did not want to see his brother's death over and over again. At any cost, he had to succeed.

He looked to the table and stopped. The gem had changed.

The stone was red, the color of blood.

This would be the spell then—the banishment, not the containment. Not that he would tell his vampire "ally." Whatever service Eric provided could serve as some atonement for all the rest he'd done—a last act of sacrifice before George destroyed him.

Blood was the way.

The gem would not lie.

Xander felt Cordelia shiver in his arms. It looked like she was on the verge of tears.

"I don't think we should go out there," she whispered.

Whatever was going on outside that doorway sounded extremely violent. If Dave was anywhere near as good as Ian, he knew how to take care of himself. But who knew what he was facing?

"I think we have to," Xander replied. "Two people went out there because you sent them there."

"Xander Harris!" Cordy sputtered. "I didn't . . . I mean, I wouldn't . . ." She stopped. "It's gotten quiet."

She was right. The shouting and banging and growling had gone away. It probably hadn't lasted a minute. But it had sounded awful.

"I can't stand it," Cordy said. "I've got to look." She grabbed Xander's hand and rushed up the stairs.

They found Dave on his knees, attending to a fallen Barb.

"We heard something out here," Xander said. "What happened?"

"A vampire," Dave said.

"Naomi," Barb whispered.

"Naomi?" Cordelia asked incredulously.

Xander could see the marks on the other girl's neck. "It bit Barb."

"She didn't get very much blood," Dave explained. "Barb will be all right."

"Very much blood," Cordelia whispered. She looked horrified.

Dave looked up at her. "Why did you bring us out here? Did you know this was going to happen?"

"N-no. I—I—" Cordelia sputtered. "I don't remember!"

Dave stared at her for a moment before nodding. "No, you do not. There is great evil here. If there is time before the spell begins, we'll talk to my Uncle George."

Xander had other ideas. "Well, okay, but first we have to talk to a couple of friends of ours. It's time for Buffy and Giles to help us figure out what's going on."

Gloria strolled down the alley once the human kids were gone. The place was actually beginning to feel homey. Sure it was filthy, it smelled, it was full of rats. But it was their filth, their smell, their rats.

Tonight, she guessed she just felt good about being a vampire.

She and Bryce had gone off to a little hidey-hole she knew—a hidey-hole that even Naomi hadn't found—and there she had taught Bryce some very important lessons, things that were both nice and nasty. That was one advantage of being a vampire—the nasties were of a more varied sort. She had certainly enjoyed it, and she thought Bryce had too, even though he wasn't exactly the talkative sort. Oh well. Gloria did enough talking for two, anyways.

And they had done it all right under the nose of know-it-all Naomi.

Gloria giggled. "Naomi says this. Naomi says that. I wonder what Naomi would say if she knew what we were doing? Hey, Brycie?"

Bryce lumbered into the alleyway. The shuffling creature was many things, but he wasn't fast. *Ah well,* Gloria thought. *In some things, slow is good.*

She had had some trouble convincing the big lug to leave this alley, even though her hiding place was only a block away. He had appeared uncomfortable. He had grunted, hesitated, urged her back toward the alley.

"Ah, Brycie," she had cooed. "You just aren't comfortable away from home?"

But still he had followed. And once Gloria had him in her lair, he hadn't made a single move to leave.

"Didn't we have fun, Brycie?" She had already asked the question a dozen times, but it was worth asking again. "Gloria had fun. You may not be much to look at, but there's a spirit deep inside there. Gloria knows."

Bryce made a choking sound.

Gloria stroked his matted hair. "Was her little muck monster afraid? Naomi's nowhere around. She never missed Gloria. She never missed Bryce. She'll never know."

"Hu—hu—hu," Bryce managed.

Gloria clapped her hands. "Are you trying to tell little Gloria something?"

Deep within the hair and filth, she thought she saw Bryce nod his head. "Hu—hurt."

"A word? Gloria thought you didn't have any words. See what being with Gloria can do for you? Already you're talking!"

Bryce nodded again. "Hurt. Hurt Naomi."

"Really? Yes. I think we can hurt Naomi." She clapped her hands again. "Gloria has an idea! I think we'll pretend to serve her for awhile. Be real nice to her. Gloria can do that. But Brycie says to hurt her, then we'll hurt her. Nobody talks to Gloria like that!"

"Hurt," Bryce mumbled one final time, then shambled back into his place behind the dumpster.

Gloria supposed she should go to her place, too. She was supposed to be watching Cordelia. After all, Naomi said so.

Gloria would have her little life, but it did no good to make Naomi angry. At least until she could help Bryce with his little wish. Except Gloria would make it even better. She wouldn't just hurt Naomi.

She wanted to kill her.

Chapter 16

IAN!" TOM CALLED FROM THE OTHER ROOM.

What was it now? He'd barely gotten back to the rented cottage, and already his brother was shouting for him.

Not that their uncle could bother to lend a hand. He should have been supervising all of this, but he spent almost all his time staring at that crystal of his. Uncle George had always been a man of moods, but since their father had died, and especially since they had come to Sunnydale, all of his moods had been bad. Ian and his brothers had taken to keeping out of his way unless they absolutely had to talk to him, and their uncle hadn't objected.

So, until the real spell began on the following evening, it was up to Ian and his brothers to get things moving. He had come back with the latest bundle of merchandise that his uncle had wanted for his incantations, mostly arcane herbs from a store tucked very far out of the way. Apparently you could find anything in California, as long as you knew where to look. He'd be eternally grateful to Oz for showing him around.

In fact, Ian had already told Oz to pop on by. Not everybody had to be as secretive as his uncle. And with any luck, they could at least pass Oz's lycanthropy problem by their uncle. Maybe Uncle George couldn't fix it now, but once they'd dealt with the Hellmouth, a werewolf-reversal spell would be a relatively simple matter.

Just another day in the life of a Druid. Ian had run errands while Tom—if anyone in the family had inherited their father's gifts, it was Tom—concocted the spell. Their other brother, Dave, had avoided their uncle entirely and gone out to be with some new girl he'd met. It was all right with Ian; the minor spells they were producing now could be watched over by one or two people. *Well, no,* now that he thought of it, *it isn't all right.* He wished he could have gone with Dave. He wished he could see Buffy and this time go right up and tell her how he felt.

Ian sighed. If his uncle ever learned of his feelings for the Slayer, George would have far more than a bad mood. Druids, after all, were supposed to stick with their own kind.

"Ian!" Tom's voice was getting frantic. "I'm really serious! Something is going on in here!"

Ian put down the bag of supplies and ran for the bathroom down the too-white hall.

Tom was tending the early forms of a potion they planned to use as part of the greater spell. Ian almost laughed when his uncle told him where they were going to concoct their brew. When the builders of this quaint little place put in the bathtub, they probably never envisioned that it would someday contain a noxious liquid intended to save the world.

He found Tom waiting at the bathroom door.

"What's the matter?" Ian asked.

"I can't leave the potion," Tom replied. "Uncle's given us specific instructions."

"Is this a problem?" Maybe, Ian thought, his brother wanted to join Dave.

"No." Tom pointed into the bathroom. "The problem is in there. Whatever's in the tub—I think it's alive!"

Ian pushed by his brother and walked into the room. He stopped some three feet away from the bathtub. Something, indeed, was happening within.

The tub appeared to be filled with a dark green, viscous fluid. Little points of light shimmered on the surface whenever it was still. But it was not often still. The deep green liquid would roll and heave in a most agitated fashion, for perhaps a minute at a time, and then quiet for a few seconds, as if it might be gaining strength to begin again. Sometimes the liquid looked to be filled with air bubbles; at others, there appeared to be small, hard lumps swimming just below the surface of the dark green fluid.

"Is this supposed to be happening?" Tom asked.

"What is it?" Ian had never seen anything quite like it. It certainly didn't look like anything they had done before.

"It's the same brew you left me with—the preparation for the vegetation spell, to help seal the Hellmouth."

"It can't be." That was one of the ancillary spells their uncle had decided would help back up the primary magic. When they had performed a practice preparation at home, three inches of liquid had swirled around the bottom of a basin.

Perhaps there was some miscalculation involved here, something their uncle had changed to deal with the power they were facing. He looked back at Tom. "Did Uncle tell you to make a larger batch?"

Tom shook his head. "This is the exact same spell we used before."

"What could be different?" Ian asked, the answer coming to him before the question was fully out of his mouth.

"The Hellmouth!" he announced. But if the proximity of a point of power made that much difference to this simple incantation, what would it do to the great spells his uncle planned to use?

"This is very troubling."

"Well," Tom replied, "it *is* only a vegetation spell."

But, Ian thought, *that's the very reason this was serious.* And where was his uncle, anyway? He should be right in the middle of this sort of thing.

"Hey."

Both Ian and Tom spun around to see Oz standing just outside the bathroom door.

Tom looked at the mess in the bathtub and almost smiled. Well, if he was going to be more open about what they were doing, this was a good place to start.

"The front door was wide open," Oz said with a wave, "and this was obviously where things were happening."

Tom nodded. "I think you could say that."

"We seem to have a little trouble with our bathtub," Ian admitted.

Oz stepped between them to get a better view. Both eyebrows went up as soon as he looked at the tub. "Wow. Now that's a hair clog."

"No," Ian replied, "this was something we planned to do—well, sort of. We were putting together a little something to help in our uncle's big fight against evil."

Tom shook his head. "Yes, except this particular something never moved on its own before."

Oz squinted at the bubbling mess in front of them.

"I think this particular something's trying to get out of the tub." He looked at the two brothers. "Is this anybody you know?"

Ian saw that Oz was right. The mass in the tub was heaving up and down even more than it had before. And parts of the mass seemed to heave above the tub in an almost recognizable shape. Some parts looked like tentacles, or maybe even arms. Oz was more than right. It was exactly as if something in that oozing mass was trying to find a way out of the tub.

"Any*body?"* Ian heard a note of panic in his voice. "This shouldn't be moving!"

"Well, hey, we can take care of that." Not fazed in the least, Oz walked past the brothers and opened the doors under the sink. "Uh-huh," he said after a moment's pause. "This'll do just fine."

He pulled out a plunger, then turned to look at the very active liquid in the tub.

"You've got to watch it for a minute," he told the others.

Oz was right. The thing in the tub did have a pattern. The middle of it would heave up, then the arm/tentacles would form to either side, then back to the middle again. It was getting noisier as it moved about, too. At first, Ian didn't notice much but the expected sort of sloshing sounds. But he had begun to notice a lower, grumbling noise going on underneath.

Maybe Oz had seen something like this before. But, in all his years of Druid training, Ian never had.

"You've sort of got to get into the right rhythm," Oz explained.

"Oz, wait!" Ian called. He and his brother were the spellcasters around here. They should be figuring out how to deal with this.

Oz dodged a particularly long feeler. "I think it suspects."

The feeler receded into the tub and rose once again at the center.

"Now!" he cried and hit the top of the heaving mass hard with the plunger.

The mass paused as if in shock, then made a great moaning sound, collapsing in the middle like a soufflé that had the air knocked out of it.

No one moved for a long moment.

The liquid in the bathtub was still.

What had Oz done to the spell? Ian looked down at the now inactive sludge.

"I don't know if you should have done that."

"I was caught in the moment." Oz grinned. "I don't know what would have happened if I didn't."

"It was pretty quick thinking," Tom added. "How'd you know to hit it there?"

"You sort of get an extra sense about these things after a while." Oz shrugged. "This sort of thing happens every day around here." He grinned. "Besides, I'm a master of drain clogs."

Ian found Oz's words rather chilling. "This should have been a very simple spell. It became far too powerful. I think my uncle has miscalculated. If the Hellmouth affects every spell in this way, this could be a potentially deadly problem. We may have to rethink everything we intend to do."

Tom looked down at the now three inches of innocent, though slimy, looking liquid in the tub. "So we've got work to do. Where the heck is Dave?"

"Dave will show up. I'm more worried about Uncle George. With the kind of row that thing was making, shouldn't he have checked in here by now?"

"I will kill them!" Naomi fumed. "I ordered them to serve me, and they were nowhere to be found!"

Bryce and Gloria had disappeared. They had left her vulnerable. Once she had become a vampire, she thought she had left that sort of thing behind. But others could still betray her. How high was the cost of betrayal to a vampire? She still needed Bryce and Gloria for a day or two. But when their plan was done, she had plans for their very colorful—well, one couldn't really call them *deaths,* now could one?

Eric smiled at her. "Servants can sometimes be so untrustworthy." He waved at the star-filled sky above them. "You have to put it in perspective. What will the two of them matter when we rule the world, and everyone serves us?"

Eric always made her feel better. He had taught her so much, really. She had only been a very average vampire before he had come along. He had shown her how to change Bryce into the thing he was without allowing him to die, and he had trained her to place the still-living Cordelia under her spell.

"So you still feel it will be the two of us?" she asked softly.

"Naomi. After all this time how can you even ask? Only together can we guarantee the plan will work. I'm the one who knows the magic. You're the one who knows the Slayer."

He put one of his strong hands on her shoulder. "But we will have to review the particulars. Tomorrow night all our dreams come true."

"Our dreams?" Naomi wanted to laugh. Eric made her feel like she was part of something huge.

"While I finish my part in this, you and the others

will have to handle the Slayer. You must keep her occupied. Even though she knows nothing of the Druids' spells, her interference could disrupt everything."

He gently turned her so they were face to face. "Our plan is in motion. One more night and all will be different."

"Different," Naomi echoed.

"Don't worry, Naomi. Eric will take care of you."

She hoped so. Eric had taught her even more than he realized.

She had tasted her first betrayal in this, her new life after death. If Eric were ever to betray her, too, her vengeance would be terrible to behold.

Chapter 17

BUFFY HEADED STRAIGHT FOR THE HIGH SCHOOL LIbrary. They met there whenever things got really bad; after all, it was sort of like Giles's headquarters. She just hoped Giles knew how bad this whole Druid thing was, and was already knee-deep in a plan.

"Buffy!" She heard Xander's voice as she was about to walk across the high school lawn. "Boy, are we glad to see you."

She turned to see Xander and Cordelia, along with one of Ian's brothers. All of them looked rather the worse for wear. "Things are not sunny in the dale," was all Xander said. "We're going to see Giles."

Buffy nodded. "Ditto on the bad. Ditto on the Giles."

They headed for the one door Giles always kept open when he was in the library. The Watcher was in.

The four of them poured into the library together. Giles and Willow looked up from where both of them had been staring into a monitor.

"I had been expecting you," Giles said in that offhand way he had.

"All of us?" Xander asked.

"Well, some of you at least," Giles admitted, glancing at Dave and hesitating. "Things are about to occur."

Willow nodded. "Either the computer program's gone crazy, or it's the end of the world." She paused a minute, then added, "I'm hoping it's the computer program."

"Well, it's not the only thing that's gone crazy around here." Buffy quickly told everybody about her battle with the plants.

"I'm afraid I recognize that," Dave said when she was done.

"So the wild grabby plants are a Druid thing?" Buffy asked.

"Yes, that's one of the spells that my uncle is planning to use tomorrow. But that sort of growth, that sort of aggression—none of that should have happened so soon. I'm sure my uncle and brothers have barely completed the preliminary incantations. If the plants react so strongly to the preparatory spells, how will they react to the real thing?"

"Perhaps," Giles mused, "should your uncle come back here as he had promised, we might be able to talk about this."

"My uncle hasn't been back to talk?" Dave asked incredulously. "From everything he'd said before, the participation of the Slayer in all this was crucial. I can't understand why he hasn't come back to explain."

Giles surveyed the rest of those who had just entered the room. "But none of you look particularly happy. Did all of you have to fend off these plants?"

"There's more than a giant green thumb out there," Xander piped up. "We've just survived a vampire attack."

Buffy shook her head. "No matter what, there are always vampires."

"Not like this one," Xander explained. "For one thing, it's Naomi."

Naomi? Buffy whistled. Ms. whining-is-a-way-of-life? Out of all of Cordelia's old gang, Buffy always found Naomi to be the most grating. And self-centered. And petty. Actually, for Naomi, being a vampire was not that much of a stretch.

"And," Xander added, "I think she's done the whammy to Cordelia."

Buffy realized Cordelia hadn't spoken once. Now this was serious.

"She's also bit one of the local girls," Dave interjected. "Luckily, I got there before she could drain very much blood. We got her a little water, a little something to eat—"

"Donuts," Xander explained. "There's not much open in Sunnydale this time of night."

"I treated the wound with a little something I had," Dave continued. "It cleared right up and we got her home. There's a few things we always carry for that kind of emergency. I could give you a list."

"I'm sure that would be very handy," Giles replied.

"No wonder the computer program's going crazy," Willow added. "For some place where nothing is supposed to happen, there's an awful lot happening."

"Poor Barb." Dave smiled at the thought of her. "I'm sure when she wakes up tomorrow, all of this will seem like a bad dream."

"It's a common occurrence in Sunnydale," Giles assured him.

"Well, that dream sort of thing," Buffy agreed. "There's a lot of stuff people around here just can't handle."

"Hey, there's stuff *here* we can't handle," Xander interjected. He quickly related how he noticed Cordelia was acting a bit strangely, that she was insisting a young woman—Barb—should go out in the back alley behind the Bronze, a back alley where Naomi waited. And then, as soon as she had gotten Barb to go out there, Cordelia forgot the whole sequence of events.

Giles rubbed the bridge of his nose under his glasses. "I believe that would be a mastery spell. Cordelia? Do you remember any of this?"

Cordelia shook her head miserably.

The librarian did not seem in the least surprised. "Yes, that would be in keeping with this sort of control. I'm quite certain there's a way out of it. I'll have to do a little research. In the meantime, Cordelia, stay close to the others. I'm sure, if Naomi tries to snare you again, the others can pull you out of it."

Cordelia nodded. She didn't look very convinced. *Mostly,* Buffy thought, *she looks very scared.*

"Okay," Xander said. "Somebody's got to ask this question. Is there any way this vampire stuff fits in with the plants?"

Giles considered for a moment before he answered. "In Sunnydale, who can say?"

"Around here," Willow piped up, "vampires are a part of *everything.*"

"Precisely."

"Vampires R Us," Buffy agreed. "Well, unless I can stop them."

"With the additional problem," Giles continued, "that, as we can see, the Druids' own magic is threatening to go out of control."

There was a moment of silence. *Even with the extra help,* Buffy thought, *we're still overwhelmed.*

"Well," Giles said at last, "now that we're all here, we should do something about this."

Xander nodded. "If we could figure out exactly what 'this' is."

"Has anybody seen Oz?" Willow asked.

"Oz and Ian were running a bunch of errands," Xander replied.

"Well, maybe Uncle George will explain something to him," Dave ventured. "After his insistence on working with you people, I just can't understand what's happening."

"You and everybody else in this room," Buffy agreed.

George knew now what he had to do. He had left the cottage quietly, without a word to his nephews. But he kept the crystal in the inside pocket of his coat, close to his heart.

He could feel the stone vibrate through his cotton shirt. The power of prophecy was returning. Perhaps the Hellmouth was recharging the crystal too. The stone would be there to help him when the moment of decision came.

It was time to deal with the Slayer and her friends. He should have spoken to them long ago. How long had he sat in that room, listening to his past? The memories had kept him rooted to the spot.

How odd, he thought, *that Eric had followed me here.* But he was grateful to the bloodsucker in a way, for Eric's appearance was really what shook George from his torpor.

Now his senses were reawakening. Bits of power

were coming back to the elder Druid. He could hear birds call on the other side of town, feel the heat of the stars on the back of his hand. He could sense the gatherings of souls in the buildings before him and could hear those no longer alive moving together at the center of town.

But the Slayer and her friends—he knew they were all together. But with one of his nephews? How did that come to be? He could no longer read the more subtle of signs. The world around the Hellmouth was becoming more unsettled with every passing moment.

George searched the room around the Slayer. Yes, she was there, too.

Only moments before, the red had drained from the stone, and the divining crystal had begun to speak to him at last. The crystal had told him that she was the one he needed. But it was so obvious, really.

He had been blinded by remorse. He would be blind no more.

What would he say now when he finally stood in front of them, not a projection, but in the flesh?

He was certain he could put them at their ease. He no longer knew if he wanted to expend the energy. Explanations meant nothing. What mattered was the success of the spell. There would have to be a sacrifice. More than just blood. For the spell to succeed, George would have to sacrifice a life.

Any human life would suffice. Pity it had to be one of the Vampire Slayer's friends. But, if her friends were involved, the Slayer would be involved, too. It was simple and efficient.

George smiled.

He would succeed at last.

Chapter 18

BUFFY WAS GLAD GILES PUT HER EXHAUSTION INTO words.

"It's late," Giles said, "Everybody should go home and get some sleep. Tomorrow we may be up all night."

"Tomorrow?" Cordelia shouted like she had been shaken from a deep sleep. She looked at the others in horror.

"Tomorrow? But that's the night of the Spring Formal!"

"It's also the night that, according to my uncle, the forces of evil must be prevented from taking over the world," Dave added helpfully.

"How considerate is *that?*" Cordelia took a deep breath. "Well, I guess this affects me, too. Especially considering what's been going on with Naomi." She winced, saying the next few words as if every one had to be dragged from deep inside. "The Spring Formal is out."

She pointed her index finger at her boyfriend. "But, Xander Harris, we're going to every single other dance that Sunnydale High ever holds!"

"Ever?" Xander echoed.

She frowned slightly as she paused to consider. "Well, at least until graduation. After that, we'll see."

Buffy decided there was hope for Cordelia yet.

"Come on, everybody," she called to the others in the room. "I'll walk you home."

Willow looked up from her computer monitor. "Giles? Do you think we should look into this mastery business?"

"Oh, right. That is rather important. Willow and I will be doing just a bit more work." He nodded at their resident computer genius. "If it's all right, I'll give you a lift."

"Hey, anything to defeat the forces of evil." She waved to the rest of the crowd. "If you see Oz, tell him I'll give him a call!"

Buffy thought Willow looked a little sad. As busy as she was, Willow might be feeling lonely. With all that had been going on the past couple of days, the usually inseparable twosome of Willow and Oz had been pretty separated.

But they all had their part to play in this. The rougher the situation, the more Willow stayed glued to the computer. Buffy wondered if other Slayers had

had such a wonderful network of friends to help them out.

People were pretty quiet as they walked through the streets of Sunnydale. She guessed everybody was tired. The streets were quiet, too, as if even Sunnydale was resting. *Getting ready,* Buffy guessed, *for tomorrow night. The end of the world. Again.*

She left Cordelia and Xander at Cordelia's house. Dave waved and said he had to get back to see his uncle.

Buffy had no choice but to head for home. The Slayer was all alone once more.

Xander had never seen Cordelia so jumpy. Every rustle of leaves, every insect chirp, had her grabbing for him, which he sort of liked. But her constant gasps and yelps ended up startling him, too. It was even making him a little panicky.

He put his arm around her and walked her firmly up the steps to her front porch. Cordelia searched in her purse for her keys, never a short procedure at the best of times.

She frowned up at Xander. "What if I wake up in the middle of the night and Naomi's staring at me?"

Xander wished that he could calm her down. He squeezed both her shoulders.

"Hey. Remember there's no way for a vampire to get inside unless you ask them in."

"You're sure about that?" She pulled out her keys at last.

"Inside. I'm here. I'll make sure that nobody's around until I hear you lock the door behind me. Willow and Giles are still working on this. Between them, they can get to the bottom of anything. I'm sure we'll be able to figure a way out of all of this tomorrow."

Cordelia sighed. "I hope so." She took a final glance over Xander's shoulder at the dark, dark world. "I'd better get inside."

Big brave Xander. And what happened when Cordelia had locked the door and he was out here all alone? Well, Buffy was probably just down the street. No doubt she'd show up if he screamed loud enough.

Cordelia gave him a goodnight kiss that was barely a kiss at all. Xander could tell that her heart wasn't in it.

She unlocked the door quickly, but paused as she stepped over the threshold to look back at Xander a final time.

"And I'm going to miss the Spring Formal!" she wailed.

The door shut behind her. Xander waited for the sound of the bolt being turned. He went down the steps and headed for his own house on this very quiet night.

He stopped and took a look around. It was spooky how empty the streets were.

Why did he feel like he was being watched?

He wondered if it was too late to drop in on Ian and the others for those promised Druid lessons.

It would be so easy for Naomi now.

She could wait until Cordelia was almost asleep. Cordelia's oh-so-cute, oh-so-sincere boyfriend, Xander, had said that vampires can't come inside when they're not invited. True, as far as it went, but it didn't matter. Naomi could just call Cordelia back outside.

Naomi remembered back when Xander was such a skinny nerd that Cordelia wouldn't look at him twice. My, but the boy had filled out nicely. Naomi imagined he'd be quite tasty, too.

She had toyed with putting Cordelia back under her spell tonight, or with attacking Xander on Cordelia's front porch, draining him and leaving him for Cordelia to find in the morning.

But both plans lacked drama. It was far too quiet in Sunnydale now. Naomi's best plans deserved an audience. She would wait until tomorrow, when she could use Cordelia, when she could use both of them as part of the larger drama that would swallow Sunnydale whole. Naomi pictured the perfect moment. She'd let Cordelia regain her consciousness just long enough to watch Naomi drain the life's blood from her precious Xander. And then, why not let Eric drain Cordelia to give him extra strength to defeat the Druids?

It was a lovely plan. She was sure Eric would appreciate its poetry.

But enough of Cordelia and her little high school chums.

Right now, Naomi had other business.

So Buffy was feeling sorry for herself. So what?

Well, Cordelia and Xander were gone in one direction, and Dave down a different street to check on Barb and head home. The march of the dancing couples. Only Buffy was destined to march everalone.

Angel . . .

Sorry, sorry, sorry.

"Buffy!"

Two young men waved at her as they ran up the street. Oz—and Ian.

"Have you seen my uncle anywhere?" Ian called.

"She looks like she had a fight with your spell," Oz added. "Sorry, Buffy. You all right?"

"No prob." She tried to smile at Ian. "Just a little run-in with killer plants." Oh yeah, the torn clothes, the smudged face, the too-tangled-for-a-comb hair. She always liked to run into prospective dates when it looked like she had been rolling around in fertilizer.

Oz pointed down to his less-than-spotless clothing. "We had to put down the revolt of some bathtub goop, ourselves. You haven't seen Willow around?"

"Sure. Willow's still at the library. We just left there. Willow and Giles are still doing that—you know—computer stuff."

Oz nodded. "Maybe I'll just drop by." He pointed at Ian. "Tomorrow?"

Ian nodded back. "We can use all the help we can get."

Buffy was glad Oz was going to drop in on Willow. She thought that would be good for both of them.

She was even happier that it left her alone with Ian.

Oz trotted off down the street in the direction of the high school. Ian smiled kind of shyly. *A good first sign,* Buffy thought.

"I haven't talked to you much," he said

"Yeah. I kind of noticed. I figured it was because of the Druidic silence and all."

"Yeah, we Druids have that kind of reputation, don't we?"

There was a pause in the conversation.

Well, Buffy thought, *now that we've covered the social habits of Druids, where do we go from here?*

"So," she asked, "you're looking for your uncle? So was Dave."

Ian shrugged. "Yeah. He's acting a little strange. More than a little, really. Here we are, ready to turn back the tide of evil that's seeping through the Hellmouth. This is not a small thing."

"Not small at all," Buffy agreed. "Actually sounds kind of big."

"It couldn't be bigger. According to my uncle's calculations, if this thing isn't stopped by tomorrow night, it could change the world."

"And this change isn't a good thing, right?"

"It couldn't be worse. My uncle was really hyper about this whole thing until we got here to Sunnydale. Then, all of a sudden he gets into one of these moods—my uncle has these moods; you'll have to take my word for it. And so he just sits in the living room and broods. Oh," Ian pointed off someplace behind him, "we rented a cottage out by the edge of town. Anyway, my uncle said it was very important that we enlist your services. Gives us a little extra help in case anything goes wrong."

"Well, he did visit Giles once," Buffy offered.

Ian looked up to the sky. "And that's it! Did he ever mention any of the finer points of his plan?"

"I don't think he ever mentioned his plan."

"Exactly." Ian sighed. "And then, after totally screwing up his own schedule, tonight he simply disappears, without a word. There's something very strange going on in the Hellmouth."

"Understatement of the year," Buffy agreed.

After a moment's pause, she added, "Maybe Giles could help you find your uncle. He's good at that sort of thing."

Ian considered that for a moment before answering. "No, if my uncle doesn't want to be found, no one will find him. That's another Druid sort of thing."

Wait a second.

"But," Buffy pointed out, "if you won't find him, then why are you out looking for him?"

Ian threw up his hands. "Well, I had to do something!" He looked at his hands, as if surprised they were in the air. He grinned a little sheepishly. "Besides, I was sort of hoping that I would run into you."

Buffy found herself grinning, too. Now that Ian was talking to her, he said nice things.

"So what are you doing this fine middle-of-the-night?" Ian asked.

"Me? Actually, I was headed home."

Ian nodded, and looked around at the empty streets. "Well, since I have absolutely no idea where he's gone, I guess I could look for my uncle in the direction of your house."

"It sounds like a plan," Buffy agreed. After a moment, she added, "It would be nice to have someone walk me home for a change."

"Always glad to oblige."

So they walked.

"Even though we come from different traditions," Ian said after a moment, "I feel . . . a great . . . affinity for you."

Affinity? Buffy thought. *Well, that's new.* Not necessarily bad. Just new.

"Are we all that different?" she asked after another silence. "We're both looking for the same things."

"And we use some of the same methods. You're a great fighter."

"Thanks." Buffy was glad it was the middle of the night. She thought she was blushing. "You're no slouch yourself."

"Just think, if the world was a different place, like

a comic book or a TV show, we'd make a great crime-fighting team."

"Yeah," Buffy agreed. "*If* the world was a different place."

She looked up. They were already at her place. Didn't this walk usually take longer?

"Well, this is it," Buffy said. "The old Summers place."

"I really enjoyed talking to you."

Somehow, they were facing each other. Somehow, they were only a foot apart.

"Yeah," Buffy said, looking up at Ian. "I enjoyed talking, too."

"We'll have to do it some more. Not that I'm supposed to be here all that long. Maybe we can do something tomorrow."

"Yeah," Buffy said. "Tomorrow." Half an hour ago, she wasn't even sure she was ever going to see Ian again. Now, she was half hoping he would kiss her.

"Of course, tomorrow might also be the end of the world." Ian grinned. "I suppose it'll give us something to talk about."

"I'm glad you finally told me something about why you're here. I really wanted to trust you." As long as the two of them kept talking, and standing here like this, maybe, just maybe . . .

"We want you to trust us, too." Ian frowned. "What was my uncle thinking about?" He looked up toward the house. "I've really got to find him."

"Find him," Buffy repeated. The spell was broken. She glanced toward her front door, "Well, look, I've really got to go inside."

"Yes." He waved as he trotted away. "We'll talk tomorrow."

"Tomorrow," she echoed.

Wow. She wasn't exactly sure what happened there.

At this rate, if they had a couple of weeks, this could grow into a real romance.

And when was he leaving? Probably as soon as his uncle finished his spell? And when was that? Tomorrow?

Like usual, Buffy girl, your timing is perfect.

Buffy sighed and unlocked her front door. She really needed her sleep.

One way or another, tomorrow was going to be a big day.

Willow kept such thorough files on their earlier cases that it only took a few minutes to get some really meaty descriptions of the mastery spell.

She scrolled quickly down through the text.

"Ooh, there's a lot on this, but most of it's very old."

Giles looked up from the pile of books he was perusing. "Interesting. I can't find any recent mention of it either. It appears to be a power or a spell that some vampires once controlled, but most seem to have lost. Drusilla's name keeps cropping up, though. I wonder if she used it in her fight with Kendra. It would certainly explain how easily the vampire killed a Slayer."

"Yeah. Maybe they don't use it very often," Willow mused as she skipped on to the next likely Web site. "Maybe the knowledge was only used by certain vampires. Most of these references I have are central European. You know, the classic vampires."

"European, hmm?" Giles stroked his chin. "I wonder if the Druids brought something with them—oh, unknowingly of course."

"I never meant to bring any vampires."

"Pardon?" Giles said. Both Willow and he looked up at the sound of the new voice.

It was George, the elder Druid, standing just inside the library door. And this time, Willow noted, he cast a shadow.

"But a new vampire did follow me—that is, from Wales," George continued. "He makes offers of power, offers of control." He shook his head. "I'm afraid this Hellmouth is a very confusing place."

"Especially for an outsider," Giles gently agreed. "We are willing to assist you." *Assuming you tell us what's going on* . . . he added silently.

"I have been remiss in not seeking you out earlier." He spread his palms, face up, in a gesture of helplessness. "I am afraid there have been certain complications."

"There always are." Giles sighed. "I think we can thank the Hellmouth for that, too."

"Yes. Well, I'm afraid that my needs have changed . . . in a way that you may not approve." George looked directly at Willow.

Giles frowned. He stepped quickly in front of the Druid. "Willow, get out of here!"

"I'm afraid it is too late for that," George said.

Giles raised a hand to block the other's way, but his hand froze and began to shake as though it was fighting against an invisible force.

"Hey!" Willow called from behind the computer. "Giles?"

"You do not make it easy," the Druid said to Giles. "But you cannot stop me."

Giles's whole body was shaking now. "If you—do this you are—no better than those—things you fight against!"

George smiled sadly as he stepped past the librarian. "You might be right. And after I have successfully completed my spell, you or the Slayer will be free to destroy me, if you still so choose. But I will have served my purpose, and I will die content."

The Druid sighed as he slowly approached Willow. "I had been blind for so long. Blind to the truth that our only chance lies in the ancient rituals, the spells of life and blood." He held out a hand toward Willow, as if he was asking her to be his partner in some ancient dance. "As I should have seen it as a sign that this woman was named after our beloved Willow tree."

"No! N—" Giles's voice stopped abruptly. He no longer shook. He seemed frozen solid.

"I hope you will forgive me," George said to Willow, "but he was becoming tiresome."

Willow stood up, backing away from her computer. "What do you want me for?" she offered in a shaky voice. "I'm just the computer girl. I can be far more useful to you in gathering information. What do you want to know?"

"I'm afraid the time for information has come and gone. There's now only time for action."

There had to be some way she could distract him. Maybe she could still get away.

"You're going to leave Giles as a statue?"

"Oh, you're right. It would be easier to just put him to sleep."

George nodded toward Giles without turning his gaze from Willow. The librarian moaned and fell gently to the floor.

"Willow." George smiled gently. "I can not think of a more appropriate name for what must be done."

Willow looked around. The Druid had her backed against a shelf of books. "Uh, I think I really should be staying here—"

"I'm sorry. That is no longer under your control." He frowned for an instant as his index finger touched his brow. "Willow—Rosenberg, that is correct? You are about to do a very important thing. You are about to save the world."

Oh, Willow thought. *That didn't sound so bad.*

"I promise you there will be no pain."

That however, sounded worse. Willow did not like any sentence that included the word "pain."

"Wait!" she called.

George shook his head sadly. Lightning seemed to leap from his fingers.

The room went blinding white.

Where is Buffy when you need her?

Chapter 19

NAOMI HAD BEEN WAITING FOR A MOMENT LIKE THIS all her life, and all her death. She had told the others to meet her here, out by the packing plant, in the most desolate part of town. Here, they could make their plans without being disturbed.

Naomi stood on the open loading dock, a natural stage, and waited for the rest of her kind.

Many of the vampires had left town when the Druids arrived—many, but not all. And others had come to take the absent ones' places. The Hellmouth drew the undead to its power, like insects to a flame.

She saw the others gather on the broken asphalt before her. These were not the vampires with dreams of conquest, these were the everyday vampires, the car mechanics and college students and surfer dudes and housewives and high school nerds.

Naomi had turned a few of those last ones herself. They were so easy to attract, so desperate for her bite. She so enjoyed having a half-dozen four-eyed geeks who had aced chemistry now under her spell.

Perhaps they weren't the brightest vampires. Perhaps they weren't the most socially adept. But these vampires had a quality Naomi deeply admired. For to these vampires, Naomi was a queen.

Eric had seen to that, giving her the full vampire makeover. Under his instruction, she had gone from high school chick to irresistible ice maiden in one easy lesson. He had given her depth and mystery and power.

Naomi glanced down at her pale hands with their perfectly formed, blood red nails. Who would have thought it would take her death to make her a real woman?

"Come out my children!" she called, eager to hurry them along. It was time for the final speech, and the final plan.

And so they came, emerging from their basements and back alleys, crypts and coffins, still wearing the mechanics uniforms and aprons and letter sweaters that had been a part of their former lives. These were the little people—sorry, the little *vampires*—perhaps a hundred of them or more, who would make all of Naomi's dreams come true. She noticed with approval that Gloria and Bryce were there as well. She was glad she wouldn't have to use any extra energy to hunt them down, but could let them walk blindly into her retribution.

"My children!" she announced as the parking lot filled with undead. "Your wait will soon be over! Tomorrow is our night."

That got their attention. A hundred pale faces all looked up to her.

"Tomorrow, we will complete a spell in which evil will triumph forever! No one will ever look down on you again! In the new world, you will reign supreme."

Eric had never exactly explained how this was going to work, but she trusted him, at least most of the time. Would he have helped her so much, done all those nice things, if he was then just going to turn around and dump her?

She only knew one thing. Soon, a whole new world would open up before her, and she and Eric would be at its very center, filled with the power of the Hellmouth!

Whatever that was.

But her audience was waiting.

"We are so close to victory!" she continued. "So I want you to meet here again, an hour after dusk tomorrow. We must fight one great final battle, to ensure that our kind will be triumphant—forever! And then, on every night between now and eternity, we will have our pick of the living! They will kneel down and offer themselves to us, grateful for our attention!"

A great murmur rose through the crowd. They liked that idea. She did, too. She hoped it was something like what would actually happen.

"So gather your strength!" she told her audience. "Prepare your thirst. Tomorrow we face the Slayer, all of us together, so that we might tear her limb from limb and feast on her bones!"

"Feast on her bones!" someone cried in the audience.

"Feast on her bones!" she repeated, and the audience repeated it with her.

"Feast on her bones! Feast! Feast! Feast!"

She waited for the cheer to die out, then shouted one single word. "Tomorrow!"

Naomi stepped back from the edge of the loading dock. She had no illusions. Her followers would engage the Slayer tomorrow and divert her attention from Eric's business. But her followers were untrained. They would eventually overwhelm the Slayer with their sheer numbers, but not before many of them had been destroyed.

Oh well, Naomi thought. The spell will have worked by then. Eric will be triumphant. And there will be that much more for those vampires still around.

Her audience began to drift away. But she still had business with two of them.

"Gloria! Bryce!"

The two waited as the others disappeared.

"Come here!" she called. Both of them slowly approached the loading dock. Gloria seemed to be wearing some sort of fuscia gown. From its hideous cut and color, it must once have been worn by a bridesmaid. Where did Gloria find these things? She couldn't tell what Bryce was wearing, which Naomi supposed was just as well.

Naomi waited for both of them to be immediately beneath her before she spoke again.

"Where were you two earlier tonight?"

" 'Tonight?' she says." Gloria looked confused. "What time was that?"

Naomi wouldn't let Gloria slide out of this that easily. "Earlier tonight. I told you I would need you!"

Gloria looked over at the thing that had once been Bryce Abbot. " 'Watch over Cordelia,' she says. 'Don't let her out of your sight.' " She glanced back at Naomi. "Is that what you're asking Gloria?"

She was right. Naomi had said that. Could Gloria have actually been obeying orders?

Well, she had given no such conflicting commands to her muck monster. "Where was Bryce?"

" 'Where was Bryce?' she asks. Bryce is still mortal. Maybe Naomi forgets that. Sometimes, Gloria thinks, Bryce needs to go and do things. Find food and water. Find a place to relieve himself. Is that right, Bryce?"

"Hu—hu—hu," Bryce said.

Naomi was talking to two idiots. Maybe, Naomi realized, she had told Gloria to be somewhere else. And with the thing that used to be Bryce Abbot—when one took away most of somebody's humanity, maybe a certain amount of intelligence went with it. Very well. Perhaps she would not threaten them just yet.

But, when tomorrow night was over, she would kill them anyway.

Gloria waited to make sure Naomi had floated away somewhere. She waited until all the sounds of the night—birds, rats, and insects—started up all over again. Those sounds all went away whenever groups of vampires got together—as if any self-respecting vampire would eat insects!—and would only come back when the creatures thought it safe.

"I guess it's safe to talk, Brycie," she said at last, shaking her fist at the loading platform where Naomi had stood ten minutes before. "Well, isn't she Miss High-and-Mighty!"

Gloria jumped up on the platform, ready to do her best Naomi impression. She strutted back in forth. "My children! Tomorrow—I give you—everything! And all you've got to do is kill—a Slayer! Someone who only destroyed the Vessel, killed the Master, trashed the Order of Taraka! What a bargain!" She looked down at Bryce. "Pretty good, huh?"

"Hu-hu," Bryce agreed.

"Just who does she think she is?" Gloria went on. " 'Wait a minute,' she says. 'I want to talk to you two,' she says. And we have to bow and scrape to her every word!"

"Hu—hu—hu," Bryce agreed.

Gloria smiled at the thought. "Yes, Brycie, Gloria will help you put pretty little Naomi in her place." She stared at the loading dock where Naomi held court. " 'Where were you tonight,' she says. 'I needed you,' she says. Oh, if Naomi knew where Gloria and Brycie were, she'd be more than mad!"

"Hu—hu—hu."

She jumped down from the platform and gave the muck creature a playful shove. It made a squishing sound where she hit it. "You do have a one-track mind, don't you, you naughty boy?

"But we can save that for later. Now, Gloria's got a plan. Naomi thinks she can tell Bryce and Gloria whatever she wants. Naomi thinks she's got it all figured out.

"Well she won't be quite so high-and-mighty if Buffy finds out about her plans. That's what Gloria says!" She looked around to make absolutely sure that the two of them were all alone. "Now listen to me, my prince of muck. Gloria and Naomi both have to sleep during the day. But Brycie doesn't have any such problem. This is what I need you to do—"

"Hu?" Bryce asked.

She considered her companion. "You're not very good at passing along messages, are you? Gloria will write a note."

Gloria chuckled as she searched the ground for a piece of paper. "It's payback time!"

Oz opened the library door.

He closed it right away, and stayed in the hall. The uncle Druid, George, was in there doing something that didn't look all that friendly. He heard Willow ask George if he was going to leave Giles like that, caught a glimpse as the door swung closed of the librarian slumping to the floor. He could hear muffled voices coming through the now closed door. Willow did not sound at all happy.

Oz quickly reviewed his options. Of course, he wanted to rescue Willow. However, it was his guess that Giles had already tried to rescue Willow, and Giles was currently slumped on the floor. Therefore, direct confrontation might not be the best answer.

One thing was clear: this not-too-friendly thing George was doing seemed very different from anything Ian or the other young Druids had told him about. What if they knew what their uncle was planning, and were lying about it the whole time? Oz made a fist. Nah, Oz had spent too much time with the younger Druids. Something would have come up about this whole plan . . . somewhere. He doubted Ian even knew anything about George's plans. Whatever was going on here, old Uncle George was doing it on his own.

But Ian was out there looking for what Oz had just found. Oz wished he could go out and find the young Druid. Whatever Uncle George was doing, Oz had the feeling that Ian would be on Oz's side. But, if he went and got Ian, what would happen if neither of them could then find George—or Willow? Oz had to have priorities here. And Willow was number one.

Strange light flickered through the small round windows in the library doors. George was doing something magical in there, and he had to be doing it to Willow! Oz had to fight back another impulse to run right in. *Remember the slumping Giles. Think, don't punch.*

Okay. Back to those options. Sooner or later, George had to leave. Oz was standing outside of the only door. Now, the Druid could also leave by a window, but in the middle of the night, in a school where he thinks he's all alone? Why would he bother?

So it was likely that the Druid would come back through that door, maybe with Willow, maybe without. If the Druid was alone, Oz would go check on Willow. If the Druid had Willow with him, Oz would follow both of them. Once he figured out where the two of them were going, he'd find Buffy, or Ian, or maybe both of them. That's where the punching part came in.

Well, it sounded like a plan. But it didn't give Oz much comfort. Who knew what was going on in there? The weird lightning flashes had stopped, but now he could hear a low noise coming from inside the library, a sound like a mournful wind.

Something banged on the other side of the door. Oz decided he was a bit too much in the open there in the hallway. He ran as quietly as his sneakers would allow to a spot some twenty feet away, to where another hallway cut across the first. He could hide behind the water fountain there and wait to see what happened.

He heard the library doors slam open as soon as he was out of sight. The moaning wind was louder.

Now that the sound was no longer muffled by the library doors, it sounded like a hundred human voices wailing in pain. Oz could see a yellow glow coming from around the corner, too. He risked a look.

The first thing he saw was Willow, floating in the air, surrounded by the yellow, ghostly glow. She looked like she was asleep—probably another part of the Druid's spell.

George was directly behind her. All his attention seemed focused on the floating body before him, as though keeping Willow in the air took a great deal of concentration.

Oz wondered if he could risk a sneak attack while George was so involved. Well, he'd have surprise on his side for a moment. But what would happen when that moment was over?

George waved a hand. The next set of doors were flung open before him, hitting the walls with a loud bang. Oz jumped back out of sight.

Or, Oz reasoned, he could not be suicidally brave and stick by his plan—follow them, find out where they were going, and then get reinforcements. Since he'd thrown his lot in with Buffy and her crew, they'd defeated all sorts of supernatural menaces. But they'd always done it through teamwork. The Druids' arrival had sort of broken up the old gang. Both he and Xander had been spending as much time with Ian and his brothers as they had around their usual haunts. Now, though, it was probably time to get the troops together again, and maybe add three young Druids besides.

Oz realized he was making a lot of assumptions here. The three young Druids seemed like real people, but maybe they were honor bound to obey their elder, no matter what evil scheme he had in mind. Maybe, by going to Ian, he wouldn't help Willow, but end up getting himself caught as well.

Nah. Druids or no, Oz knew people. The three young Druids might have some family issues, but in the end, he hoped he could count on them to do the right thing.

Doors slammed somewhere else in the school. From the sound, George was moving fast. Oz should probably start following faster, too.

He could see a dim yellow glow receding down the school's central corridor. Oz walked rapidly after it. He heard another set of doors slam. Three sets of doors in the main corridor—that meant they were going outside. Oz hurried his pace. If, suddenly, George decided to, like, fly himself and Willow away, Oz wanted to at least know which direction they were headed.

But when he reached the front door, the two of them were only halfway down the sidewalk to the street. So he'd trail Uncle George at a safe distance. At least she was floating slowly enough for Oz to follow. Not to mention the ghostly light—it was hard to lose someone when they were surrounded by ghostly light.

George walked over to the back of a brightly painted van with the words Rent Me This Weekend! $19.95! He opened the door and mumbled a few words. Willow floated into the back.

Well, this wasn't as bad as Druids flying away, but a van could lose Oz all the same. He waited for George to climb in the front, then sprinted from the school down to the rental.

The van had an unused roof rack on the top, the kind you used to tie up extra mattresses or furniture. It would have to do.

Oz climbed on the back bumper of the van, and grabbing onto the rack, hauled himself up to the roof as the Druid started the engine. It sometimes seemed odd that Druids would use modern devices like cars. Oz guessed he had always seen—if indeed he ever thought about it—them as sort of like the Amish, only with magic. Now they were driving around. They had probably even taken a plane to Sunnydale! It just reminded him how little he really knew about these people he'd only met a few days ago.

Oz felt the van beneath him jerk into gear. He didn't have any more time for thinking. The only way he was ever going to rescue Willow was if he could manage to hold on.

Well, they were going somewhere, just not fast. This looked like it could take all night. Hey, who needed sleep when the maiden of his dreams was in danger?

He'd find where old George was taking her, then figure out if he could sneak in or had to go get help.

He'd figure out some way to save the day, whether he had to face magic or not. After all, he was pretty handy with a plunger.

The van began to gain some speed and went over some speed bumps faster than maybe the driving Druid should, each one rattling the van and jerking Oz's arms at the shoulder sockets. Maybe George was just not very experienced driving a van. Maybe he was just planning to drive very badly.

But George's driving didn't matter. All Oz had to do was hang on for dear life.

Two lives, really—his and Willow's.

Chapter 20

THERE WAS SO MUCH FOR GILES TO DO. MORE WAS happening in Sunnydale every day. He had been reading police reports of vandals out in the graveyard tearing apart coffins. It appeared to be getting worse from one night to the next. And then George had come to him with the story of another crisis, something that might affect the entire world.

He had so wanted to trust George. Buffy and her friends were wonderful helpers, but they were young and simply didn't have the accumulated perspective on life. To have another adult with whom he could work—well, there had been Jenny, but it was so painful to think about Jenny.

Giles was walking. Where was he going? He was going to find George.

This isn't real, Giles realized. When had he fallen asleep? When had he started dreaming?

He came to a deserted concrete room—a part of some old factory perhaps. George was there.

"Help me," George said.

How could he? Giles remembered that George had done something very wrong.

"Help me," George called again. Giles saw there was another, darker figure behind the Druid, a figure lost in shadow, all but his pale hands, which were clasped on George's shoulders, holding him in place.

"No," George said. "No. You and yours will create a distraction. You and yours will help end the terror. But I must finish this myself."

The Druid, the room, the mysterious figure—all were gone. Giles wanted to wake up.

Why couldn't he wake up?

George had to do it. He had to.

No! Don't let them nearer! Don't let them!

The failure of all their work. The failure of his brother's spell. The failure of his spell.

He had to make up for everything, not just in front of the boys, or before the other elders, but in front of the world.

The stone had showed him the way. He had looked within its facets and seen blood. He was not close enough to the ancient symbols. To triumph, they all must return to the ancient ways.

In a sense, this whole past year had been a dream. He had lived with the visions, every moment of every day. For months, he had only wanted to shut them out. Now he wished to embrace them and make them his own.

He had lived his brother's death over and over again. But worse than that. He had tried to block the images that had flooded him in that instant before his brother's passing. He had seen the other side. Even now, he could not find the words to express what he had witnessed—the overload on his senses, the cries of fury, of panic, of despair; the feeling of corruption, of an evil more powerful than anything he had ever known; a million faces, two million hands, all trying to drown him in their midst.

Eric was a vampire. George knew about vampires. This was much worse than vampires. Vampires could drain your blood; they could turn you into a creature without a soul. But these creatures would tear apart his immortal soul throughout eternity.

No! Don't let them nearer! Don't let them!

He relived the moment, dreamed the dream. Sometimes in the dream he was his brother, screaming for salvation. In those dreams, part of him wanted to let them come. He needed to be punished for his failure. He needed to be punished for making the wrong choice. He needed to be punished for letting his brother die.

The agony was waiting. Perhaps, in the end, he would offer up his soul to save the world. But it would be a form of redemption. He could have a new life, and an honorable death.

It had all begun with Eric. George had been woken by a vampire. Eric had found him nearly a year ago, after the failed spell. Eric said he had been drawn to the blood in the magic.

They had had conversations from time to time thereafter. Eric was beyond morality, reprehensible—yet he was so old and wise in his way.

Eric was the first to tell George of the Hellmouth. It was the strongest of all the points of power, yet its true nature had been hidden from the Druids until they had employed the proper counterspells to reveal its deceptive nature. And Eric had helped him in so many other little ways.

George had thought himself rid of Eric when he came to this side of the world. When the vampire had first appeared, George had been horrified, afraid that he would never be rid of him.

Now he sometimes found the vampire's presence oddly reassuring.

He planned to use Eric, the same way he was sure Eric planned to use him. Any cooperation would have to be very short-lived, and monitored carefully.

Desperate times called for desperate measures. Eric would be used to dealing with average humans. He would have no knowledge of the depths of power and strength available to a Druid.

So he would use the undead. And so he would kill to protect the living. He hoped, in the end, that his nephews—and the elders of his order—would forgive him. They'd see the truth when they were living in that better world.

He remembered how Eric had surprised him at the cottage. How had the vampire found his way in?

Permission from an earlier occupant perhaps. That was the problem with a rental: you had no idea who had been there before you.

Then again, it could have something more directly to do with the Hellmouth. The rules were different this close to the center of power.

The Hellmouth was playing havoc with his basic skills. Ever since he reached the high school, he could swear he was being followed by a werewolf. A werewolf? The moon wasn't even full. The odd sense stayed with him even after he began driving the van, all alone on the streets of Sunnydale.

He would be glad to be done with this.

He looked in the rearview mirror and spoke to the floating girl in her trance: "I am sorry, young lady, but your death will usher in a whole new world."

Now why had he done that? Mostly, he guessed, to hear the sound of his own voice. He was grateful for any noise that might break the darkness.

The spell might have closed Willow's eyes, but her brain was still working. She felt like she was drifting in a swimming pool, except, of course, this particular pool didn't have any water, and her obnoxious cousin Ronnie wasn't splashing her at every opportunity. But she had that same weightless sensation.

The Druid George had silenced Giles with a single look, then done this to Willow without too much more effort. Oh, there had been some business with lightning jumping from his fingers; Willow couldn't exactly remember it. Or maybe it was more that she couldn't make sense of it. That was a problem with magic; many times, on the surface, it didn't appear to be very logical.

Well then, brute force was out, not, frankly, that Willow ever considered that much of an option. But Buffy was pretty good in the force department, except—in this case—by the time she had gone into the windup for one of her fabulous flying kicks, George would have turned her into a stone or tree or something.

But, even though they'd never faced Druids before, they'd faced other nasty things. Some probably even nastier. There had been a way out of everything else; they had won out over all sorts of creatures—the Master, the Annointed One, Moloch, Angelus. Why would this be any different?

If Willow had been awake, she would have sighed. If only she knew what was going to happen.

Of course! She did know what was going to happen. Sort of.

Willow thought about the prophecies. She had studied them often enough, as much to try to determine how the computer program had come up with the darned things as anything else.

The first one went:

"There is a shift in the undead. There exists a potential for a gathering of vampires."

Well she didn't think that had anything to do with the Druids. Well, unless that was what the Druids were fighting against. They had spoken of a "Great Evil." But it didn't look like any of them had come forward to tell them exactly what the Great Evil was. Vampires were bad, but they hadn't been anywhere near as awful as some of those world-destroying demons Buffy and the gang had had to face.

If anything, the first prophecy was only a small part of the answer. The second one went:

"A new wave will sweep the surface clean. Beware of those lurking below."

Were the Druids the new wave? And was Uncle George lurking below? She supposed it fit, sort of. If George was running around with a secret agenda, and he had kind of knocked Giles out and now was taking Willow who knew where—she guessed that counted as a secret agenda. But it didn't seem very lurkinglike. Well, at least not now.

The final paragraph on the computer printout had read:

"A single night will mean the difference. The power could change everything."

Well, that was probably why she was getting abducted. The program was trying to tell them about the importance of power on a single night—the night George and the Druids were going to perform their spell.

The prophecies still seemed to go from the ridiculously general to the specific but vague. Neither one of the extremes was exactly very useful.

Well, if she or any of them lived through tomorrow, maybe they'd figure out if the prophecies meant anything at all, and she'd save herself another twenty years of work trying to figure them out.

Actually, working for twenty years on a computer program sounded very good right now.

But maybe the prophecies would show her some other way to free herself. Maybe George would let her talk, and she could wriggle her way out of this. Maybe the prophecies would mean something to him. Especially something to make him stop.

Hey, it was worth a try. If they still meant "sacrifice Willow," she hadn't lost anything, had she?

Maybe she could put George to work making sense of all of it. She wondered if Druids ever used computers?

She heard car doors slam and another thump above her, in between the first door slam and the second, like something landing on the roof of a car. An engine started up.

So George was taking her somewhere, inside something? This floating around didn't give her much information at all.

The engine was a gentle purr. She would float forever.

An old children's rhyme drifted into her head:

Row, row, row your boat,
Gently down the stream
Merrily, merrily, merrily, merrily,
Life is but a dream.

Row, row, row . . .
Drifting, forever drifting . . .

The voice brought her back from her deepening dreams. She was drifting away from reality. Reality? The only reality she had was in her own head.

It was the Druid's voice. What was he saying?

"I am sorry, young lady, but your death will usher in a whole new world."

Oh yes, her death. Well, it was nice of the Druid to confirm her suspicions.

Her death. That was why she had to stay awake.

The engine purred in her ears.

Her death. That was why she had to plan.

Row, row, row your boat.

Nothing but floating.

There had to be some way out of this.

Gently down the stream.

Surely someone would find Giles. He would tell them what happened.

Merrily, merrily, merrily, merrily, merrily.

What else could she do? She was lost in darkness, with only the soft roar of a car—or maybe a truck—or maybe—or—or . . .

Life is but a dream.

Oz was still hanging in there. And the van, while not exactly speeding, was moving along at a steady pace.

Sometimes he thought the werewolf thing gave him extra stamina, even when he wasn't the hairiest thing in Sunnydale. He could easily outlast his bandmates, practicing for hours. And when he did decide to take a test—he'd promised his mother he would graduate some day—he could stay up all night studying and still be able to read the test paper the next day. And, so far, he'd managed to hold on to the aluminum bars of the luggage rack over some pretty impressive bumps.

At least they kept to the back roads. George probably wanted to call as little attention to this rental van as possible. They'd driven in sort of a circle around the center of town, heading for the new developments out beyond the cemetery. Briefly, Oz thought George might be heading for the rented cottage. But the van roared on by the entrance to the development and traveled maybe another half a mile before it turned at last onto a short gravel road that dead-ended in front of some old concrete warehouse.

Oz jumped from the van as soon as it stopped. He was still more or less in one piece. The way his arms felt, though, they could be three inches longer than when he'd started this ride. The Druid turned off the engine as Oz sprinted to the nearest hiding place, a set of rusted gas pumps in the middle of the parking lot.

Instead of opening the back of the van and retrieving Willow, George walked directly to the warehouse.

Uh-oh. Decision time again. Should Oz try for the big Willow rescue, or should he see what George was up to?

It was time to review his options one more time. First, the Willow scenario:

What would he do if he opened the back door of the van, assuming it wasn't locked, and Willow was still floating? Push her home? And how could he hide that eerie glow? He supposed he could have stolen the van if he knew how to hot-wire a car. Guys in movies always knew how to hot-wire cars. For one fleeting moment, he wished he had taken auto shop instead of music.

No, he didn't. He took music to get away from those guys in auto shop.

He decided it was time to take Door Number Two. George had walked into the warehouse and left the door open behind him. There was someone else inside—Oz could hear voices.

Maybe if he listened in, it might give him some clue what to do next. This, he realized, might not even be George's final stop with Willow in the back of the van. Heck, before the night was done, Oz's arms could be six inches longer.

He ran to the side of the building, careful to crouch below window level as he approached the open door. The voices grew clearer as he approached. He could start to make out the words.

"See?" one of the voices was saying. "Isn't it everything I told you it would be?"

"Yes, Eric, it is close to the source, it has a great deal of room, and there's a place to lock up our sacrifice."

Sacrifice? Not that Oz hadn't suspected something like that, but his heart sank just the same. Now he really had to get Willow out of there!

"I have influence in certain circles around here," Eric went on. "I got the electricity turned back on."

"It will save me from having to use illumination spells," George replied. "Thank you. I don't think I'll be using the electricity directly—"

"I know more about your magic than you might imagine. It's amazing, if you have a few hundred years, how it helps you to catch up on your studies."

"Please don't remind me of your vampire past. This is a simple agreement!"

"From which both of us benefit."

"It ends tomorrow night."

"Oh yes, it ends tomorrow. But by then the world will be a very different place, for both of us." Eric chuckled. "I will take my leave."

"When we see each other again," George insisted, "it will be as enemies."

"Then perhaps we never need to see each other again."

Oz saw movement inside. *Whoa!* Someone was coming out. He scrambled to get out of sight around the corner of the building.

The Eric person said he would be back later; there were still things that he had to do. George reluctantly agreed, saying they could start being enemies tomorrow night.

Oz hadn't seen any second vehicle outside the warehouse. He wondered how Eric had gotten there and how he was leaving. He hoped he wasn't walking by Oz's particular corner of the building.

They spoke about tomorrow night. Oz guessed

Willow would be safe until then. Did he dare look at the setup inside? Well, maybe just a peek. But then Oz had to get the reinforcements.

Whoever this Eric was, along with George, they were going to have to deal with Buffy.

Buffy walked alone. Where was she? The shapes of town were gone, replaced by the vaguest of shadows.

She saw a streetlight before her. A figure dressed in black waited underneath. He smiled, showing his fangs.

"I've been waiting for you," the vampire said. "You may call me Eric."

"I may also call you dead." Buffy reached for the bag, but she didn't have it. Where had it gone?

"Things are not that simple," Eric said.

Buffy frowned. "Things don't seem to be real."

"Then this could be a dream?" Eric still smiled. "People can die in their dreams, you know."

She heard Willow's voice, calling her name. Willow sounded very far away.

"You won't be able to save her," Eric said. "You're already too late."

"If this is a dream," Buffy shot back, "I could just wake up!"

"You could, if you were in control."

"And who's in control?" another voice called from Buffy's side.

The smile fell from the vampire's face. "What are you doing here?"

Buffy turned to see Ian standing beside her. He winked at her.

"I'm a Druid," he said. "Druids are very good with dreams, you know."

Eric seemed to be completely undone. "How can you do this? You don't have the power!"

Ian smiled at Buffy. "Who says that I'm the one who is doing this? After all, this vision at my side is the Chosen One. But why is she having this dream in the first place?" He turned to stare at Eric. "Could it be someone is attempting to intimidate her, to fill her head with doubt so that she might make the wrong move at a crucial moment? Oh, Eric . . . how you underestimate the Slayer!"

Buffy grinned at Ian. "If this is a dream, all I have to do is dream up a tool or two."

A wooden stake appeared in her hand.

"I will not allow it!" Eric shouted. "You can't do this!"

"Sure she can," Ian replied pleasantly. "Slayers can do anything." He looked to the vampire again. "How little you think of those who oppose you, Eric. It will be your undoing."

"You pitiful children!" Eric growled. "You may be able to influence her dreams, but you cannot change what is meant to be!"

"And what exactly *is* meant to be?" Ian countered.

"I think a vampire was meant to be staked." Buffy ran forward, weapon in hand.

Eric vanished, leaving only an angry roar behind.

Ian whistled. "Most vampires are cowards, aren't they?"

Buffy looked at the boy, somehow once again at her side. "Are you for real?"

Ian shook his head. "This is a dream. I'm not even sure how I got here, or if I'll even remember this in the morning. But I'm glad I had a chance to see you, even like this."

"Well, yeah," Buffy agreed. "I'd like to get to know you better, even if it's in a dream. Maybe we could—I don't know—go vampire hunting together."

"Vampire hunting is only one of many things we share. I know what it's like to be an outsider. We have a lot in common, Buffy Summers."

She was in his arms. She wanted to be in his arms. He leaned forward for a kiss.

Buffy woke up.

What did *that* mean? Well, it was a dream, but a dream not entirely of her own making. Part of it came from a vampire. Part of it, maybe, from Ian.

How much came from inside herself?

She blinked and looked around the room. It was early morning, maybe half an hour before her mother normally got her up for school. Sunlight was already streaming through the blinds of her window.

But what about the dream?

The dream told her the end of this business with

the Druids was very near. Maybe Willow was in danger.

She'd have to get up and find the others. Maybe Giles could figure out what the dream meant, if she could figure out any way to explain it.

Buffy sighed. Her lips still wished she had slept for a few seconds more, at least until after the kiss.

Chapter 21

SHE WAS SAFE DURING THE DAY. CORDELIA HAD TO keep telling herself that fact through her morning shower, the brushing of her teeth, the one glass of orange juice—the only part of breakfast that she had wanted. She told herself again as she hurried up the walk to school. She was safe during the day.

It was only at night that Naomi could call out to her.

But if Naomi called her again, how could Cordelia keep from doing something terrible? Last night, Cordelia had tried to get poor Barb to go into Naomi's clutches. No, it was worse than that; she had sent Barb to be bitten by a vampire. If Dave hadn't been there, Barb would have been dead. Or worse. All because of Cordelia.

And she couldn't remember any of it.

It was like Naomi was using Cordy's brain without

her permission. As if there was an extra somebody creeping around inside of her skull.

Cordelia barely kept herself from shivering. Oh, she hoped Giles and Willow had turned up something last night!

"Hi, Cordelia!"

Cordelia almost jumped out of her skin. But it was only Amanda, waving at her from the high school steps.

"So, tonight's the big night!" Amanda enthused.

"The big night?" Cordelia asked, not quite connecting. Had Amanda heard something? She pulled open the door as Amanda fell into step next to her.

"For the Spring Formal, silly!"

"Oh, right, the Spring Formal." Cordelia tried to smile.

"So did you tell Xander what kind of corsage to get? You can't have it clashing with your dress, and these boys are so helpless when it comes to fashion stuff."

Cordelia stared at Amanda. How could she have ever felt that any of this was important? Well, no, it would be important any time but now.

Should she tell Amanda about it? Who was she kidding? Amanda? But Cordelia wanted to tell her something.

She shook her head. "No—well, I don't think I'm going."

"What? After being on the planning committee? Did you and Xander have a fight?" Amanda looked outraged. "I think you should go without him."

Wouldn't you just love *to see me show without a date?* Cordelia thought, then sighed. "Yeah, I guess there was a fight. And Xander and I still have to work things out."

"You're going to work things out rather than go to the Spring Formal?" Amanda shook her head in astonishment. "Sometimes, Cordelia, you can be so weird."

Amanda was right. Right now, Cordelia was weird.

But it wasn't her fault. She had to keep reminding herself of that, too. Naomi had done something to her, something that Cordelia was going to change.

With Willow's and Giles's help, she'd take that "weird," and stuff it right down Naomi's throat.

"Listen," Amanda said abruptly, "I've got to stop in here for a minute."

Cordelia looked up. She was having trouble today paying attention to her surroundings. They were right in front of the door to the girls locker room, a couple of classrooms away from Cordelia's locker.

Boy, she hoped she didn't see Naomi's face in the mirror again.

"Well, see you!" Amanda called.

She opened the door to a whole bunch of screams.

She let the door swing shut.

"Maybe," Amanda said, "I don't have to go in there right now."

Well, that nails it, Cordelia thought. *Another crisis. Should she do something?*

Two girls burst from the room, one wearing street

clothes, the other rapidly buttoning a blouse over her gym shorts. From the looks on their faces, they wanted to be anywhere but in that locker room.

"What—," Cordelia began, but neither one of the girls stopped long enough to chat.

What was going on now? No doubt something incredibly icky. Was Buffy in trouble? Buffy gravitated to icky. Maybe there was some way Cordelia could help. Maybe she should go get Giles. Cordelia sighed again. Why couldn't she just go to some school where the real crisis *was* whether or not you went to the Spring Formal?

"Is anybody in there?" she called.

One more girl hurried past her, still pulling on her T-shirt as she ran out the door. "You don't want to know what's in there!"

The swinging locker-room door flipped back and forth. The smell hit Cordelia first. She had smelled that odor before. It had something to do with Naomi.

"Ewww," Amanda complained. "Did something back up? Like the entire sewer system of Sunnydale?"

There were noises coming out of the locker room, a banging and a scraping. "Something's moving in there." She heard a crash, as if a whole row of lockers had just toppled.

Amanda laughed uneasily. "Who needs gym? Even better, maybe I'll go to lacrosse practice wearing my Anne Klein skirt."

Another crash. Cordelia took a step away. Amanda took more than a few steps away. A couple other girls had shown up, too, but no one particularly wanted to be the first one to go into that locker room. Cordelia noticed that no one was particularly leaving either. It was sort of like passing an accident on the highway . . . you didn't really want to look, but you sort of did.

She heard a groaning noise on the other side of the door.

"Hu—hu—hu."

The door swung open.

All the girls in the hallway screamed together.

A muck monster stood framed in the door. Most of the other girls took off. But Cordelia couldn't. There was something . . .

An instant later, Cordelia realized she *knew* this creature!

The whole thing came flooding back. Naomi had introduced him and suggested various unspeakable things—some kind of threat against Cordelia. Most all of it seemed like a threat against Cordelia.

Now Naomi had sent her servant!

So Cordelia wasn't safe during the day! But she was in school, surrounded by her fellow students. What could the forces of evil do when it was almost time for the homeroom bell?

There had to be some way out of this.

Cordelia waved at the monster.

"Bryce?" She tried to smile. "I know we meant something to each other once. But—keep away. No matter what Naomi says, I just don't think we're compatible."

"Ewww!" Amanda shouted from where she had stepped a dozen feet down the hall. "You know this thing's name?"

"We all know this thing. He used to be called Bryce Abbot."

"That's Bryce Abbot?" another of the girls asked. "Ugh. He must have stopped taking showers."

"I heard college can change a person," someone agreed.

"What does he want?" somebody else asked.

That, Cordelia realized, *is a very good question.* Since he'd shown up in the locker room doorway, the thing hadn't made a single threatening move. In fact, it hadn't made much of any moves at all.

"What do you want?" Cordelia asked.

"Hu—," he said.

"He's trying to speak!" Amanda called.

"Sla—sla—," the monster replied.

Cordelia thought she could see Bryce's eyes under all that matted hair. If she recalled correctly, they had been very nice eyes. He wasn't going to attack her. If anything, he looked scared of her and all the other girls who hung back at a distance.

There was a piece of paper in his hand.

She almost jumped back as he thrust it forward.

"Sleigh!" he rumbled.

Sleigh? Slayer? This was for Buffy? She took the crumpled piece of paper. It was a little on the slimy side, too. "Sure. I'll make sure she gets it."

"You *understand* this thing?" Amanda demanded.

"Slade?" asked someone else.

"Who the heck is that?" asked a third.

Cordelia shrugged. "Oh, it's just the—uh—nickname of a friend of mine." She smiled at the monster as she backed away. "Thanks, Bryce. I'll make sure she gets it."

Amanda nodded in approval. "Slade. Sort of a cool name. Is she part of a motorcycle gang?" She glanced up at the locker room door, which was once again swinging to a close. The muck monster was gone. "But how did you know that was Bryce Abbot? Boy, Cordelia, are you weird!"

Cordelia decided she had had enough of Amanda for one morning. She looked down at the crumpled paper in her hand. There were words written between the muck stains. It was a real message.

"How did I know it was Bryce?" She glanced up at Amanda. "You never forget a boy you dated."

"Ewww!" all the other girls agreed.

The voice of authority cut through their chatter.

"All right! What's going on here?"

Cordelia hastily stuck the note in the front of her sweater. She knew what was coming before she even saw the principal.

Principal Snyder was a small, nervous, balding man with a penetrating stare. The first time he looked at you, *every* time he looked at you, there was something in his expression that said you were guilty.

Cordy had spent the last few months actively avoiding Snyder. She hadn't gotten into real trouble at Sunnydale High for at least the last three principals. That was probably close to two years around here. Endless hours in the after-school detention hall? No, thank you. She had better things to do.

"Well?" the principal's voice cut through her thoughts. Guilty, guilty, guilty. Whatever was going on here, Principal Snyder would put an end to it. Principal Snyder could put an end to anything.

"I was about to go into the locker room," Amanda said, "when all of a sudden there was all this screaming."

Principal Snyder nodded curtly.

Well, if this was in the hands of the school administration, Cordelia had other things to do.

"See you later, Amanda."

Cordelia found herself caught in Snyder's unforgiving gaze. "Where do you think you're going, young lady? Cordelia Chase, isn't it? Nobody's going anywhere until I get to the bottom of this. Wait here until I come back."

Was *this* fair? She was the one who had calmed everybody down, including a certain football star turned muck monster. Of course, how do you explain that sort of thing, especially to a Principal Snyder?

"But—," Cordelia began anyway.

The principal glared at her. One did not argue with the principal. He pushed open the locker-room door.

Amanda pointed at Snyder. "But you're—this is the girls—can you—"

"I'm the principal," Snyder snapped. "I can do anything."

They all gathered just outside the door. The smell was still there.

Snyder wrinkled his nose. "Did something back up in here?"

Nobody answered him. It was very quiet in the locker room. Cordelia realized anything could hide between the rows of lockers. Who knew what Bryce might do? He wasn't exactly human any more. Or what if Naomi hadn't sent Bryce—alone?

The principal stepped inside. The door swung shut behind him.

One did not disobey Snyder. Cordy and the remaining girls would have to wait.

The door swung open again.

Principal Snyder looked at Cordelia with his X-ray vision. "You're sure there was some man in here. This isn't some practical joke?"

Cordelia could already see herself spending all morning in Snyder's office. Guilty, guilty, guilty. "Don't ask me. Ask all of the girls who ran out of there screaming!"

Ms. Applebaum, the girls-lacrosse instructor, stood with arms folded in the next doorway down the hall, the one that led to the gym. "Nobody came out this way—well, nobody but half a dozen students. I opened the door as soon as I heard the screams."

"Where could he be?" Amanda wailed.

"Well, there's a lot of cleaning up to be done in there!" Snyder surveyed the girls before him. "I never realized young women could be so . . . untidy."

Amanda wouldn't let it alone. "But what about the—*thing* in there?"

"How could there have been a man in there?" Snyder snapped. "The room only has two exits, this hallway and the gym. Both were being watched. How could he have escaped? Through the *toilet?*"

"Ewww!" Amanda and the rest of the girls agreed.

Cordelia shook her head. "I don't think we want to know."

Principal Snyder glared at the four girls, but there was nothing he could hold them on. He gave them all a short lecture on personal hygiene, then told them they were free to go, until next time. And he would be watching them all personally from here on in.

Cordelia watched Snyder march back toward his office. Well, this was starting out to be a perfect day, wasn't it? Maybe she just needed Amanda to tell her how weird she was again.

She felt the crinkled paper inside her sweater. The note could be important. She'd better get over to the library.

Xander walked into the library. The place was even more quiet than usual.

"Shop!" He'd seen that in a British movie once.

He heard a groan behind the librarian's station.

Xander hurried across the room as he saw Giles struggle to his feet.

"Hey! G-man!" Xander called. "Are you all right?"

Giles nodded his head. "I think so." He pushed his glasses up on his nose. "It's morning, is it?"

"Maybe you should cut back on those all-nighters," Xander suggested. The librarian did not look at all like his chipper self—well, his grumpy, sort-of-crusty chipper self. "Do you want me to get the school nurse?"

Giles shook his head.

"They've got Willow," he said. "The elder Druid, George, came and took her away."

Xander couldn't believe it. "They took Willow away? Those lousy, no-good, two-timing, back-stabbing Druids? But where?"

Giles looked around, found a chair, and sat down. "I don't have the faintest idea."

"Man, I trusted those guys!" Xander looked around the room as if some book was going to leap off the shelf and give him the answer. He had no idea what to do.

Buffy bopped into the room. She was smiling for a change. Well, that wouldn't last for long.

"Hey, what's the sitch?" she called.

They quickly filled her in on the situation. George's treachery, Willow's abduction, Giles's unwanted rest period.

"So those guys just came here to double-cross us?" Xander asked as the explanation was winding down.

"I don't know," Buffy replied. "Maybe we can still trust some of them. Ian was out looking for his uncle last night. I got the feeling when I talked to him that he felt like his uncle had gone off on some crazy mission."

"A crazy mission involving Willow!" Xander made a fist. The thought of something happening to Willow was getting unbearable. Even before there was a Buffy, there had been a Willow. Willow had been his best friend forever! They were so close that they could finish each other's sentences.

"I don't want to alarm anyone," Giles said from where he now rested his head in his hands, "but I think George might have wanted Willow as a sacrifice."

"Like a human sacrifice? Like a killing-as-a-part-of-a-spell human sacrifice?"

"I'm afraid so."

The library door opened again before Xander could get *really* upset.

Cordelia ran into the room. "Oh, Xander, am I glad to see you. What just happened—" She stopped to look at the librarian. "Are you all right?"

"He had a run-in with a Druid," Xander explained.

"But I thought the Druids were the good guys!"

"So did we," Buffy agreed.

"I guess they were just hiding their black hats," Xander offered.

Cordelia frowned. "So, is Willow around?"

Giles sighed. "No. I'm afraid last night Willow was abducted by one of the Druids."

"She's been abducted?" Cordelia's face fell. "That means she'll never figure out the mastery spell. Boy, these Druids are getting worse and worse!"

She was worrying about Willow figuring out her spell? Xander wanted to throw his hands up in the air. Obviously, she didn't realize what was really happening.

"Cordy! Focus here. Giles thinks Willow was abducted to be a human sacrifice!"

"Human sacrifice? I guess that's pretty serious, too."

Well, Xander recalled, *Cordy is under a vampire's spell.* One had to keep things in perspective.

Not that Xander could see any perspective at all in vampire spells and human sacrifices.

"Only one Druid did the actual abducting," Giles added, "the elder one, George. But he is their leader. The others may be compelled to follow his orders."

Xander wasn't so sure anymore—about anything. "Has anybody seen Oz? They may have done something to him, too!"

"I saw Oz last night, with Ian," Buffy said. "Ian walked me home, but Oz left to go . . . find Willow."

No one spoke for a moment. *Willow first, then Oz?* Xander thought. *Why?*

"We must assume the worst, musn't we?" Giles grimaced. "And we must devise a plan." Buffy was already roaming about the library, gathering her bag, some stakes, a crossbow. Action girl.

"This is terrible!" Xander yelled. Maybe he was overreacting. He wanted to overreact. "Willow's gone, with her computer skills. Oz is gone—well, with his Oz skills." Actually, as Xander remembered, when Oz could be coaxed in front of a computer, he was no slouch, either. "Here we are in the middle of one of the great libraries of the occult, and I don't know where to look. Sometimes I wish one of your books would just tell us what to do!"

"Oh," Cordelia said. "That reminds me. I have a note for Buffy."

"A note?" Buffy asked coming out of the weapons-locker. "From who?"

Cordelia frowned. "Well, you see, there was this muck monster in the girls locker room. Well, I used to know this muck monster, well, he wasn't a monster, then, he was a football player. But since he knew me, or he used to know me, I guess he trusted me enough to give me this. When he gave it to me, he sort of said "Slayer" so I guess it's for you."

She gave Buffy a meaningful look. "Anyways, this note, I put it away for safe keeping. Prinicipal Snyder showed up and, you know. . . ."

Buffy nodded as if she understood.

Cordelia reached into the top of her sweater.

She glared at Xander.

"Excuse me?"

Xander raised his hands in helplessness. "Well, how was I supposed to know where your hand was going?"

Cordelia rolled her eyes. Sometimes Xander was

such a *guy*. She pulled a particularly soiled peace of paper out of its hiding place. She turned back to Buffy and passed the smudged and crumpled note.

Buffy read it aloud. Xander still looked over her shoulder.

SLAYER—

BEWARE OF THE ATTACK AT THE PACKING PLANT TONIGHT. IT'S AN AMBUSH. LOOK FOR ERIC. HE'S THE DANGEROUS ONE.

A FRIEND

"A friend?" Xander couldn't quite comprehend this. "Buffy's got a friend who's a muck monster?"

Cordelia shook her head. "I don't think Bryce, or the thing that was Bryce, wrote this."

"So you and the muck monster are on a first-name basis?" *This* was the Bryce she had been talking about? This shouldn't be making Xander so upset. Right now, everything was making Xander upset.

"Xander, please," Cordelia said, "I'm going through enough already."

"Actually, I don't think I can be jealous of a muck monster." He waved at the note. "Hey, I'm surprised a muck monster can spell at all! Considering, he *was* on the football team."

"Now, Xander," Buffy broke in. "I'm sure Cordelia's got all sorts of things you don't know about." She frowned. "Whoops. I think that came out the wrong way." She held up the piece of paper in her hand. "Let's get back to the note."

Giles took the note from Buffy. "This has to do with that prophecy, the one about the gathering of vampires. It may have to do with all three. The second one had to do with treachery. That could be Eric as well. Or George."

Buffy waved the note in the air in frustration. "We need to get Willow back here to help us figure these out!"

"Willow has been an invaluable resource," Giles agreed. "But we'll muddle along somehow." From his tone, it sounded as though even he did not look forward to that prospect.

"But we must get to work," Giles announced. "We have a lot to prepare for. We have been told there will be some sort of treachery, out by the old packing plant. Perhaps we can find a way to set up an ambush for their ambush, if you see what I mean. And I think someone should go and see the Druids."

Chapter 22

THEIR RENTED COTTAGE HAD BECOME A BATTLE ZONE.

"You are sworn to serve me," George insisted.

"You've gone crazy!" his nephew, Ian shouted back "That's all I see!"

George had not expected this much resistance. In fact, it had never occurred to him that he would encounter any resistance at all.

Things had been moving very quickly, and George had not had time to plan. His abduction of Willow, while necessary, came from the sort of revelation he felt he must act upon immediately.

Odd how nicely his new requirements fit in with Eric's offer of the warehouse. This had happened sometimes back in Wales as well. It seemed the vampire was able to meet his every need, sometimes even before George realized the need existed. He regretted how much and how quickly he had come to rely now on the vampire's aid, but nothing must stand in the way of what he must do after nightfall tonight.

The old warehouse was in a far more deserted district than the cottage. Even in a quiet neighborhood like this, certain lights and noises were sure to draw attention. But at that lonely concrete bunker in the middle of the night, they should be able to fight back everything the Hellmouth might throw at them without interference.

As soon as he had taken Willow, George had considered what must be done. He knew he would have to return to the cottage to retrieve the various instruments and ingredients he needed to successfully complete his task. And he expected his three nephews would bring those incantations they had already begun so that they might have some extra protection from those creatures on the other side.

Unfortunately, at least one of his nephews had another idea.

Ian stared defiantly at his uncle. "My father would have never agreed to such a plan!"

George felt a flash of anger. "How dare you talk to me about your father? I was the one who watched your father die."

No! Don't let them nearer! Don't let them!

George! George!

I was not fast enough, George thought. *Somehow, I could have saved him. I was not well enough prepared. Somehow.*

George knew. It was his own indecision, his own

weakness, that had forced them to come here, to repeat the spell all over again. If he had to be angry at someone, it should be himself.

Didn't Ian see that this time his uncle had to succeed?

The minute he had returned to the cottage, Ian knew George planned to use the blood spell. He could not hide these things from the boys, Ian in particular. He had trained them too well.

George had traveled without other elders, he realized now, because he wanted no one questioning his authority. Perhaps he really planned to use the blood spell all along. He had certainly prepared for it as well as the other.

But George would let no other elder stand in the way of his redemption.

And now his own nephew dared to object!

"We have not sacrificed a human being for close to two thousand years. It was that early need for blood that almost destroyed us, forced us underground. You and my father told me over and over how we had found gentler, more refined ways to meet our goals."

George suddenly felt very old. "That was before—last year. You have not seen what I've seen. You haven't—"

"At last, you can explain some of this to us. What *exactly* is it that you've seen?"

George opened his mouth, but no words would come out. He could not bring himself to describe it. He would break down into tears.

It would do no good for the three boys to see their elder cry.

George looked away from his nephew. "The discussion is finished. I will brook no more disrespect. You will do as I order!"

"No," was Ian's quiet reply. "In this thing, we will not."

George sighed. It had been a hellish night. He'd gotten no sleep. The sun was rising as he'd left the warehouse. He'd argued here for the better part of an hour.

What was he doing?

He saw no way around it. Sometimes, even innocents had to be sacrificed for the greater good. When Ian was older, he would understand.

Tom and Dave had kept away from the argument. The boys were only separated by three years, but Ian, the eldest, had always been their leader.

Very well. If Ian refused to join him, George would manage as best he could with two assistants rather than three.

"Dave!" he called. "Tom! Gather together everything we need. We must make preparations for tonight."

He looked at Ian one final time. "I will leave you here. The elders will deal with you when we return home."

"*If* we return home," Ian replied. "If we even survive this."

George could not help trying for the final word.

"We would be in a better position to succeed if we were all working together."

Ian only shook his head. "No. We would be in a better position to succeed if we were to follow my late father's guidance."

"Very well. We will leave you behind. I believe we can manage without you."

The two other brothers stood by the front door. They both looked most uncomfortable. George could understand. Until now, the three had done everything together.

"I'm sorry, uncle," Tom said, "but I cannot go either."

George was stunned. He was faced with a full scale revolt. He looked to the youngest of the three brothers.

"And what of you, Dave?"

Dave looked at the floor. "We are sworn to uphold the order. I will follow you, as I promised the elders back home."

George sighed. "At least one of you has a little sense left."

He looked to his other two nephews before he left.

"You know you cannot stop me."

"I can at least try to make you see sense!" Ian shot back.

"No. I think that we cannot agree. If we both survive this night, we might someday come to an understanding. I hope so."

Ian was silent.

"This night is far from over. The power hidden within the Hellmouth is my greatest challenge."

Ian answered this time. "The night has not even begun. I think that things will happen that we cannot even imagine."

George left Ian inside and helped his nephew Dave load the supplies into the back of the van.

"Let us all hope we are ready for them," George said. "And let us all hope that some of us survive."

Oz was pretty impressed by the exchange between Ian and his uncle. He always appreciated a good argument.

His family didn't have all that many any more. Actually, he didn't stick around his house enough to figure out exactly what his family was doing. But he hoped they weren't arguing as much as when he had been around.

But this argument was direct, to the point, and immediately let the guy hiding outside the window know who was on which side.

Back at the warehouse, after Eric had left—and he must have been a vampire or another Druid or something, because he was *real* quiet; Oz didn't really hear him leave—Oz had spent a couple of minutes peering through the grimy windows, trying to see Willow. He'd heard George bring her inside, but the Druid must have put her in one of the smaller rooms off the main floor, because Oz couldn't see a single floating body or ghostly glow.

He had snuck around three sides of the structure, looking for a better angle, but mostly all he could see was old George unloading objects from a large black canvas bag. Oz hadn't seen the Druid bring the stuff in there. He figured it must be something left by Eric. He couldn't make much sense out of the things George was pulling out of the bag, either—rocks and twigs and shards of glass and a couple small pouches filled with what looked like dirt. Oh well. He was sure they were deeply meaningful to somebody.

George had looked up once or twice, like he really knew Oz was around. Oz had ducked away, and George had gone back to sorting out the objects.

Oz had been thinking it was time to stop pressing his luck and scoot when George decided to go back to the van. He thought about looking for Willow and remembered how he'd found Giles. Druids wouldn't leave things unprotected. He'd end up knocked out—or worse. If he was going to rescue Willow, he needed help.

Oz decided he'd hitch one more ride. If George was going the right way, it was certainly easier than walking. And if he was going the wrong way, Oz could always jump or something.

As it turned out, George was headed straight for the rental cottage.

Well, that was one of the places Oz wanted to go.

The sun came up on their way over there, so Oz dropped off the van when George went into a slow turn at the end of the street. Oz fell into a somersault on somebody's lawn, surprised that he ended up sitting in one piece. Maybe all those years falling down in gym class were worth something after all.

He waited for George to walk into the house, then strolled up the street.

By the time he got outside, the argument was in full gear.

Now, though, George was gone. Ian and Tom were on the good guys side. And Oz had to get to work.

He strolled into the still-open front door. "Hi, guys. Mind if I use your phone?"

Ian and Tom both stared at him.

"Or not," Oz said after a minute. "You guys OK?"

Tom was the first to speak. "Uh, yeah. Listen. About the phone. We'd love to let you use it, but we can't."

Whoops. Maybe Oz had misjudged them. "What, are you afraid of betraying your uncle?"

"No," Tom added, "we'd betray our uncle in a minute if we'd think it would help Willow."

"You know about Willow, yes?" Ian asked.

"I know about Willow," Oz agreed.

"Somehow, I had the feeling that you did. Anyway, we would let you use the phone, but we don't have one."

"No phone?" Oz mused.

"No. Our uncle couldn't figure out who would want to call a Druid."

"Plus," Tom added, "to be honest, he's always been cheap."

"We'll help you if we can," Ian said. "Our kind

has been against human sacrifice for a very long time. Well, *most* of our kind . . ."

Tom nodded. "Besides, Willow's keen."

"She is that," Ian agreed. "This is not going to be easy. It might not be possible at all. Our uncle's a very powerful man."

"Maybe so," Oz agreed. "But we've got the Slayer on our side."

There would be no more rest for George.

He'd have to wait for nightfall, and Eric, to make the last of the preparations.

They'd accomplish what they could during the day, but Dave was the youngest and least experienced of his charges. Mostly, George would depend on him to fetch and carry, and perhaps to maintain one or two of the simpler conjurings.

Perhaps his brothers would have a change of heart. Anything could happen around the Hellmouth.

George had felt clearer headed this morning despite his exhaustion. The feeling that he was being stalked by a werewolf had left him right around sunrise. He still wondered what it meant; perhaps there was some other danger hidden in that feeling. It would not surprise him if the Hellmouth was indeed more powerful at night. He would have to watch for other ways the power might try to distract him tonight.

He thought then of their captive. He called to his nephew.

"Let the young lady out of the office. The key is hanging outside the door."

He couldn't bear to leave her trapped all day. Let her take a few more breaths of morning air, take a long look at the sunshine. He was a practical man, but he wasn't cruel.

Dave returned a moment later with Willow by his side. She was walking a bit stiffly, and blinked a few times as if she weren't quite awake, but otherwise looked in good shape. The resilience of youth, George supposed. Surprisingly, the young woman appeared quite calm. George had been prepared for anything, even hysteria. He found her calm slightly unsettling.

He nodded to the young woman. "I apologize for what I have to do. I have no other choice." He waved at the warehouse around them. "I have set a spell around the perimeter of this building; no one may enter or leave without my permission. So you, Dave, and I will get to spend a few quiet hours together.

"I need—to talk—to you," Willow said, struggling to shake off the last vestiges of the spell.

"If you wish. But I will tell you now that you will not change my mind."

"I need to tell you more about the three prophecies. I have some vague ideas about what they mean, but I think they might mean a lot more to you."

"More?" George found himself interested despite himself. Prophecy, after all, was one of the gifts that the elders valued most highly.

"They come from our computer," Willow explained. "In Sunnydale, just about anything can produce unexplained phenomena."

And the computer was merely a tool, George thought, a vessel through which people chose to communicate. It seemed an ideal tool for prophecy as well.

"Would you like to hear them?" she asked.

George nodded. He could think of no reason to stop her. This was the young lady who was going to give her life this very evening to save the world. If prattling on about this made her happy, he at least owed her that much.

"The first one is 'There is a shift in the undead. There exists a potential for a gathering of vampires.'"

She paused, as if waiting for a reaction.

A new wave of vampires? Eric had told him that most of the vampires had left town. Could Eric be lying?

Druids could often tell if someone was lying, simply through noting the person's pulse, body temperature, and body language. George doubted that would work for vampires.

If Eric was caught in a lie, George would drop him; their alliance was that fragile. Unless, of course, the lie was so large that George couldn't even see it.

George dismissed the notion. Who knew the true source of this so-called prophecy or its accuracy? He was letting his personal concerns cloud his judgment.

Eric was helping him from the "inside," the side of evil, in exchange for protection from the blood spell. The vampire would not have offered the exchange if he didn't think George would succeed.

Willow continued, "The next one is 'A new wave will sweep the surface clean. Beware of those lurking below.'"

George was the new wave. It sounded so right. And those lurking below? Did that mean the creatures on the other side?

Or could it mean Eric's treachery?

George was far more unsettled than he had realized.

"Go on," he told Willow.

"Okay." She nodded. "Here's the third one: 'A single night will mean the difference. The power could change everything.'"

This was the clearest of the three. The "single night" was tonight. And he planned to use the Hellmouth's power to make basic changes in the order of things. But in ancient augury, all three prophecies within a group would comment one upon the others. The vampires, the new wave, the power—all were part of the same fabric. Each affected the other, and only by looking at all three together might you see the whole.

He realized now that it had been doubly important to find Willow. Not only was she the ideal sacrifice, but she had a message of great importance.

Her warning might even save the spell and ensure that she had not died in vain.

But were these warnings truly about Eric? Or were they somehow about his own foolishness? Was this young woman as innocent as she seemed, or did she know far more than she pretended?

That was the damned thing about prophecies. Anyone could read so much into them. These three probably all related directly to the Slayer and had nothing to do with him. And yet . . .

"So?" Willow asked impatiently.

George nodded. "They are most interesting. They could very possibly relate to tonight."

"So do they change your mind?"

"No. But I thank you for sharing them with me. They will make me far more watchful. They may help me avoid pitfalls and insure my success."

"That's good news, I guess. Well, I wouldn't want my sacrifice to be in vain." Willow's lower lip began to tremble. "Excuse me. I think I'm going to start crying now."

"I was afraid of that. Why don't you go talk to my nephew?"

George watched Willow march away. This was most unpleasant.

Ian knew they needed a plan. "We have to find some way to confront my uncle. But there's no way to tell where he's gone."

"I know," Oz said. "He's set up shop at an old warehouse less than a mile away from here."

Somehow, Ian would not be surprised if Oz knew everything. About everything.

There was a huge clatter outside, as if someone had run into the garbage cans. Xander burst into the room.

"All right!" he demanded. "What have you done with them?" He stopped and stared. "Oh, hey, Oz."

"Hey," Oz replied.

"We've got work to do," Xander said to Oz. "Giles wanted to find out what the other Druids knew."

"So they sent you?" Ian asked trying to hide his disappointment.

"No, actually, they sent Buffy. I just stopped by my house and got my old Schwinn racer so I could beat her out here."

"And you didn't beat me by much." Buffy walked in the door.

As inappropriate to the situation as it might be, Ian couldn't help but smile.

"Giles wants us all to meet back at the library," she announced. "We've got to do something to save Willow."

Tom looked doubtful. "I don't know if we can. It might ruin the spell."

Ian had deferred to his uncle long enough. "If this spell is so important, why doesn't he tell us about it? No one has practiced human sacrifice in our order for two thousand years. I think, if something's going wrong, it must be in my uncle's mind. I say we save Willow."

Tom only hesitated an instant before he nodded.

"So what do we do now?" Xander asked.

"We have all of my father's spell memorized," Ian said. "We may need to step in and fix whatever damage he has done.

"But what if Uncle George has added something he hasn't told us about?" Tom pointed out.

Ian nodded. "The Druids have never written down their secrets. We rely on memory. Because of this, my uncle has no notes. He could be planning anything."

"Giles has got a great library," Buffy replied. "Spells, counterspells, you name it!"

Ian glanced at his brother. "I think it's time the Druids learned to read."

"But what about Willow?" Xander and Oz asked simultaneously.

"Oz tells us George has got her locked up in a place not too far from here. He's bound to have surrounded the place with a protection spell. I might be able to get through it, but not without loudly announcing our presence. If we're going to barge in like that, we're going to need a plan."

"Well, Plans R Us," Buffy agreed smartly.

"And the times our plans don't work," Xander added, "we come up with other plans! Known as backup!"

"They're our specialty," Buffy agreed. "We got back."

Ian nodded. "Well, then, I guess we'd better start planning."

Chapter 23

BUFFY WAS AS READY AS SHE WAS GOING TO BE.

Night was falling.

They had spent the afternoon planning. Giles had decided they should break up into two separate units, though not the units their foes would anticipate. As he put it, "Somebody's made some very serious plans for us. If we can properly confound them, we may be able to slip them up." He had looked around the room, at Buffy and Xander, Oz and Cordelia, Ian and Tom. "We have our own unique abilities. Working together, we should be quite formidable."

Oz and Ian had taken a trip out to the warehouse where Ian's uncle had set up shop. It was exactly as Ian had suspected. Their uncle had placed a protection spell around the building. About six feet away from the concrete walls, it felt like they were hitting another wall, invisible perhaps, but no less solid.

Giles, Ian, and Buffy were planning to go up against George. Giles thought he could bumble through an antiprotection spell. If anything harder came along, Ian would have to handle it. And Buffy? Well, she was there to fight the vampire, and anything and everything that might pop out of the Hellmouth. Now that Ian had explained the connection and strengthened-bond part of George's spell, Giles began to understand the chaotic predictions of the computer program. For George to bind himself to evil, even hoping to banish it, would allow evil to bind itself to George, and thus find entry to this world. Chaos indeed.

Tom and Ian were fascinated by Oz's report on their uncle's alliance with Eric. Ian thought it explained a lot. Tom thought it only led to more questions.

While Team A attempted to stop George and rescue Willow, Tom would lead the brave volunteers (a.k.a. Xander and Oz) against the vampires. There apparently was going to be quite a gathering—a hundred vamps or more, all ready to go on a killing rampage, all to draw out the Slayer and keep her busy while the real threat unfolded elsewhere.

Tom had spent most of the afternoon instructing the two on the finer points of the crossbow. Their plan was to get in, mess up Naomi's plans, then get right back out, and let Buffy clean up the mess later. After, of course, Team A had rescued Willow.

Meanwhile, Cordelia would follow what Oz called the Werewolf Plan. Mainly, it meant she would be spending the night locked safely away. After some debate, Giles had decided to use the rare-book cage in the library for that purpose. That way, he could avoid the awkward explanations to Cordelia's parents. She'd just do the usual and say she was staying over at a friend's for the night. Besides, Giles didn't think the vampires would be looking for her here. And there would be plenty of other people around the school for the first half of the night. After all, it was the night of the annual Spring Formal.

All this, and Cordelia would have plenty to read.

While Cordelia wasn't exactly wild about the plan, she liked it better than any alternative she could think of. Xander promised to check back in with her once they'd disrupted the vampires' plans.

So they were ready to rock and roll.

"The sun is bowing out!" Xander called from his place by the window.

"Very well," Giles said. "Cordelia, I think it's time you got in the cage."

"Boy," Xander said, "I've been trying to get her in a cage for years."

Cordelia was not amused. "Xander!"

He shrugged. "Sorry. Just another example of the old Xander Harris misplaced humor. Patent pending."

Cordelia suddenly smiled. "Hey! I've got an idea!" She turned to Buffy. "Did you know there was a really happening new club over by the old packing plant? Even better than the Bronze. You should check it out."

Xander and Buffy looked at each other. "Naomi," they agreed.

Cordelia blinked then frowned. "Why'd I say that? I never go over by the packing plants. What an absolutely gross part of town." Her head jerked. "The vampires are gathering! They are going on a rampage! Half of Sunnydale will die!"

Cordelia shook her head. "Ugh. It's like I've got somebody else in my head, whose thoughts are getting all jumbled up with mine."

Her whole body jerked this time. She glared at Buffy. "Cordelia will never be free unless you confront me!"

Cordelia wailed. "Now Naomi's using my voice?"

"Into the cage, Cordy," Xander gently urged.

Cordelia quickly complied, and Giles locked her in. "I will keep one key with me. There is a second in my desk drawer. We will return here when we have completed our missions, and let Cordelia out at dawn. And I promise you, Cordelia, that once Willow is rescued, our first priority will be to lift Naomi's spell."

Cordelia nodded her head. "Xander!" she called. "I want you to be careful. I want you to let me out of here tomorrow. I want all of you to let me out of here!"

Xander nodded. "I brought my sleeping bag from home and put it in there. Over in the corner?"

Cordelia saw the old Boy Scout bag and nodded. "Why don't you get some sleep?"

"Well," Giles said. "I believe it is time to get to work."

Cordelia waved as the others filed out of the library. Buffy, the last in line, waved back.

Didn't any of these books have a plot?

Cordelia tossed aside maybe the twelfth book she had been browsing. She was doing her best not to be depressed, but the selection in here wasn't helping. Even the illustrated books seemed to feature only pictures of demons and damnation. It was hard to be stuck here, especially with the music from the dance in the gym wafting into the library. She could be out there now, looking fabulous, the envy of all Sunnydale High. Instead, she was locked in a library.

I hope nobody comes in here—

Cordelia looked up. The music faded, replaced in her senses by a horrific smell.

O—K, Cordelia thought.

She heard an all-too-familiar voice:

"So, I says, 'I know where to find Cordelia.' Oh, Cordelia!"

Now that Cordelia knew about Naomi's spell, all the other things around it kept flooding back to her. Including one that was right outside her library door.

Gloria stepped into the room. And Bryce trailed right behind her. "Sorry. I've gotta do this. Otherwise Queen Naomi will suspect. 'Get that Cordelia out here,' she says. 'She'll get that Slayer!' she says. Yeah. As soon as something goes wrong with one of her plans, she blames me. She blames both of us, right, Brycie?"

"Hu—hu—hu."

"We've gotten sort of fond of you, Brycie and me. We'll keep you out of the action if we can. It's not as if there'll be any lack of blood after all. This night *is* the end of the world." She looked around the room. "So where's the key?"

Cordelia couldn't help herself. "In the desk."

"'In the desk,' she says. This place is full of desks."

Actually, the place was full of tables. The only desk was behind the librarian's station.

"The one in the middle there," Cordelia found herself saying. "To your right. No, no, that's your left. Straight ahead now. That's it."

Gloria opened the top desk drawer and pulled out the key.

She quickly unlocked the cage.

Cordelia wished she could stay in here even as her feet were walking out.

"Look guys," she began, "I appreciate all this personal attention—"

"It's not our decision. We just got to let the whammy work—"

"Hu-hu-hu," Bryce agreed.

"Besides, we need you to get the Slayer, and the Slayer's got to be there so we can destroy Naomi."

Cordelia glanced at the muck monster at her side and tried not to breathe. Unfortunately, Bryce didn't look any less disgusting at night.

"Well," Gloria said, "what say we take another little stroll. I think it's time we gave those kids at the dance a thrill!"

Eric was afraid this was going to happen.

He had quit his adopted crypt the moment the sun dipped below the horizon. He had picked his spot carefully, close to the edge of the cemetery. Most of the other vampires residing here were not so lucky.

One of the Druids' secondary spells was already working. He had heard that it had asserted itself briefly the night before, only to disappear again by morning. Tonight, though, it was both far earlier and far stronger.

Now the cemetery was a jungle, a mass of constantly growing vines that was trapping and killing any vampire unlucky enough to be in the middle of it. As the plants grew, their tendrils became harder, and sharper, ever ready to pierce a vampire's heart. Eric heard a dozen different screams, even saw one of his kind burst into dust. There was nothing he could do. He stared at the ever growing vegetation covering tombstones and statues, trees and mausoleums, drowning everything beneath its leafy mass. If he were to reenter that jungle, he would suffer the same fate as his brethren.

Now, many of her troops would never meet Naomi. But there should still be enough to create a diversion, and a diversion was all he needed.

Eric had to be very careful about his control. It mustn't be too obvious. He couldn't dampen all the Druid spells. A few missteps could be blamed on the "influence" of the Hellmouth, but too many and George would get suspicious. George had to believe he was still master of his own fate, even though he'd lost all his power long ago.

Eric was a master of dreams. He couldn't control all the Druids, but he had the strength to influence one or two. He had observed the elders, and picked the brothers Stephen and George—both ambitious, one talented, the other envious. How easy it was to destroy Stephen and bring George under his sway. Now he would use the Druids' power to destroy everything natural, everything they loved.

The particular spell George would use was not quite what the Druid thought. It temporarily trapped most of the Hellmouth's power, leaving only a single opening brought by blood, an opening that Eric would use once he had taken over George's spell—an opening that would allow him to control the ten thousand demons and ten million damned souls that waited on the other side. None of them would get to Earth without swearing fealty to Eric. And all those he allowed through, perhaps only a few hundred at first, but thousands eventually, would repay Eric with blood and power.

The sacrifice was all that was important. All

Naomi had to do, really, was delay the Slayer. Even if she couldn't kill her, Eric would have the first of the demons by his side, any of whom could destroy even the Slayer with a single glance.

There were a few, final screams out among the leafy growth. It was a shame about the vampires. But Eric could always make more.

Naomi was not pleased at all.

Where were her hundred vampires? She saw thirty, perhaps forty, at most, milling about the parking lot before her. They should all be here by now so that she might assign them their hiding places. Had the Slayer already cut some of them off?

"Hey," a voice called from behind her on the loading dock, "we got your girl for you."

Well, at least Gloria and Bryce had come through for her. And she was going to kill them? Well, maybe she'd wait a few more hours.

"Bring Cordelia over here," Naomi said with more conviction than she felt. "I want her to see the destruction of all she loves before she dies."

She frowned as she looked out over the parking lot. A couple more pale forms had drifted in, but she could see far more broken asphalt than undead.

This was not going at all well. Where were half her troops? Had they forgotten to get up or something? Didn't they know that this was the big night, the night that was going to make Naomi forever? If she wanted Eric to love her throughout eternity, she had to keep her side of the bargain. Otherwise, he might find some new teen queen to make over into Supervamp.

Well, whoever was out there would have to suffice. All Naomi needed, she told herself, was clever planning. That, perhaps, and a little drama.

Cordelia was here. That meant the Buffy would not be far behind. This platform they stood on was very much a stage, and she was the stage manager. She'd drain Cordelia, but not until Buffy was in view. She wanted the Slayer angry and rushed, ready to make a mistake. Then her troops would descend upon her and do her in—forever!

Cordelia walked stiffly over to Naomi's side. She was once again completely under the vampire's mastery spell.

"Greetings my children!" Naomi called. "Tonight is the night we triumph! I bring before you Cordelia, whom I will drain in the presence of the Slayer!" Naomi laughed at the thought of it. "Cordelia was the queen. But who's queen now?"

The chant started out a bit on the ragged side, but gained strength with every repetition. "Naomi! Naomi! Naomi!"

Yes, Naomi thought. Why had she doubted herself? *This will work! She will triumph!*

"Naomi! Naomi! Naomi!"

Cordelia shook her head. "Oh, please? Who are you talking to? A bunch of vampires? What do they know?"

Naomi's mastery was wavering. She was letting her emotion get in the way. "Silence!" she hissed.

"You were just never good enough!" Cordelia replied. "You'd never stick to anything. You'd give it up and go on to the next thing. That's why I always beat you out."

"Naomi! Naomi!" The crowd's enthusiasm was flagging again.

"That was before I found my calling," Naomi said to Cordelia.

"As a vampire? Spare me. Sure you've got some moves. But I have some friends who will have you beat—"

Naomi had had enough of this. "You must submit to my will!" Cordelia, about to say something else, found her mouth snapped shut. Enough insolence! How could Cordelia fight her like that? Naomi had to remember Eric's lessons.

Or maybe she could teach Cordelia a lesson of her own. She didn't want to drain the young woman just yet; no, that had to wait for the Slayer. But what harm would there be in a little nip?

She heard a commotion out in the lot. She looked away from Cordelia as a long black Cadillac roared into their midst.

What was this?

Electric windows rolled down, revealing a pair of young men's faces. They had something in their hands.

Crossbows!

"Watch out!" Naomi screamed.

But they were already firing their deadly wooden bolts into the crowd.

She turned and saw Gloria hiding behind the muck monster. The bolts didn't seem to harm the large, squishy thing in the least. Gloria and Bryce were going to get away! Other vampires were fleeing, too—those lucky enough not to have been mowed down by crossbow fire.

That's what Naomi needed—a shield. And one stood only a few feet away. The hell with Eric and his plans! She had to get out of here, to suck another day.

She tugged at Cordelia's arm. "Come on." But Cordelia was frozen in place.

Naomi had no time for nuances. With a wave of her hand, she removed the spell. Cordelia sagged briefly then strengthened.

"Now you're coming with me," Naomi insisted. "And spell or no spell, I can still crush you!"

"So we're just getting a little exercise?" Cordelia looked out at the black car. One of its occupants actually waved at her. "Remember our cheerleading days together?"

Naomi couldn't help herself. "I should have been captain of the team—not you!"

"You could never be captain!" Cordelia said with a laugh. "You could never get the "Rah Sunnydale Rah" cheer right."

What was this woman saying? "I could, too!"

"You couldn't remember it for a moment!" Cordelia hunched over slightly. She was going to show her how the cheer was done? Ha! Naomi would show her!

She crouched down behind Cordelia.

"Just as the sun rises over the hill!" they shouted together. They both started to rise, doing their cheerleader imitation of the sun. "Sunnydale's gonna win! Kill! Kill! Kill!"

Naomi leaped up in the full Sunnydale cheer. But Cordelia wasn't with her. She had fallen down. Clumsy Cordelia!

Naomi looked up at a shout.

"This one's for messing with my girlfriend's mind!"

She was totally exposed. Bolts shot at her from three crossbows.

Cordelia heard a familiar voice out among the trash cans.

"Hu—hu—hu—hurt Naomi."

"'Hurt Naomi,' he says," Gloria's voice answered. "They're going to hurt us too, if we don't get out of this place, like, forever."

"Hu—hu," Bryce replied.

And then Xander was at Cordelia's side.

She was never so happy to see a guy in her life.

Chapter 24

GEORGE HAD TO PUT WILLOW IN ANOTHER TRANCE. He could not stand to look at her cry.

"I'm sorry, Uncle," his nephew David said. "I can't do this either. Not to Willow."

"Oh, no," Eric said from the doorway. "It is too late now. You will help us, or I will kill you myself."

David looked at the vampire, then back to George. "Uncle?"

"Eric is right. We must follow through on this. It may be our last chance. It has to end tonight!"

"I brought a few more things to speed the spell," Eric said as he pulled open a shoulder bag.

George was astonished as he looked inside. "How do you know so much about this?"

Eric smiled. "I thought by now it might be obvious. Come. Let us get started. I shall tell you as we go."

George hurried to make the final preparations. He pulled free the sacrificial knife, nothing more than an ornament for the past two thousand years. Tonight, it would once again find its true use.

And, once Willow's blood filled the basin, the real magic would begin.

Buffy watched the two men frown at the invisible wall.

Giles frowned. "I was sure this would work."

"My uncle's spells can be very powerful."

Giles's first attempt at breaching the spell didn't appear to have done much of anything. Not that one could really tell. Short of total success, it was hard to see what sort of effect you were having on something that was invisible.

It had been doubly frustrating because as they approached the warehouse Buffy could have sworn she saw another man had entered the building. Ian didn't know the man at all. Buffy was guessing from Oz's description that it was Eric.

Ian and Giles argued over what approach they would take next. Every once in a while, Ian would steal a glance in her direction. Buffy smiled back at him. Even if there could never be anything between them, it was still great to fight side by side.

Ian threw something at the invisible barrier as Giles shouted a string of foreign words. There was a bright flash.

Buffy blinked, trying to regain her night vision. Both Ian and Giles were getting up off the ground.

"Well, that was rather more dramatic than I had expected," Giles allowed.

"Yes," Ian replied. "But did it work?" He thrust his hand forward. It stopped as though it had hit the same invisible wall.

Buffy couldn't help herself. "Willow's time is running out!"

Giles nodded. "I know. There's got to be something that we can do."

"But what?" Ian asked.

George chanted the primary spell, Eric the secondary.

They stopped. All the preparations were in place. It was time for the sacrifice.

But by now, George knew the answer. "You have not simply studied the Druids. You are a Druid yourself."

Eric nodded. "I was one in life. And I have maintained many of the skills that I have learned there."

"I should have realized, when you came to me that night when I had not invited you—"

"Yes. I had projected my image before you."

"Something that I have done hundreds of times." George shook his head. "Little wonder then that you see the importance of our work."

"Little wonder," Eric agreed.

"But we should begin. The time is drawing near."

Eric glanced at David, watching them silently

from the other side of the room. "What about your nephew?"

George waved away the other's concern. "He will not participate, but he would not dare to interfere."

"As you wish."

Dave left the room. His uncle wished he could make the young man understand.

But it was growing late. George had to make the sacrifice. "Come. It is time for us to change the world."

Giles was lost in his books. Ian was simply lost in thought.

"Hey," Buffy called. "Look!"

Ian looked up at a broken window. "It's Dave!"

"I've disabled the protcction spell!" Dave called. "Get in here now! We need to save Willow."

The three all gathered up their tools and quickly ran to the front door without any interference.

"I had to wait until they were too wrapped up in their spellcasting to notice," Dave explained. "But since my uncle left me in charge of all the secondary spells, it was easy to shut one down. But we have to hurry! We only have a few minutes before my uncle uses the knife."

A tiny circle of light appeared before them—a pulsing, red light. An entrance to the Hellmouth. George could barely breathe.

He had seen this light before.

No! No! Don't let them near me!

The light grew, and George could hear the first faint cries of the damned, and the obscene demands of their keepers. Any of them might have the power to destroy the world. But according to the spell that Eric had given him, one had to open the Hellmouth before one could seal it.

Bursts of light came from the still-small opening, as though the things upon the other side wished to force their way through. But the opening would get no larger without the offering of blood.

George stared down at the knife before him. In a moment, he could leave all his brother's cries behind.

He picked up the knife and pricked his finger. First blood. The voices redoubled from the other side, entreating, cajoling, demanding. They wished to overwhelm him. *Soon, though, I will seal them away forever.*

The light swirled and grew—the size now, perhaps, of a tin can lid. When it was the size of a window, it would be time for the blood. The Druid chanted, and Eric joined in, drawing the power to them.

There was something wrong with the light.

It was far too red, the color of the power that had destroyed his brother—the color that had caused George to see the evil on the other side, to almost be consumed by it.

They could not control that power. It would control them.

"No!" George shouted. "The spell has gone wrong again!"

Eric smiled. "Oh, no, the spell could not be more right."

George didn't understand. "What do you mean?"

"You've never seen it, have you? This spell, all of this, has been for me all the time."

"What?" George demanded. "For you? How could this be? My brother and I—"

"Played into my hands over a year ago. This spell was never about turning back the forces of darkness. That was merely the explanation I whispered in your ear. This spell has always been to bring the powers of darkness, to bring chaos upon the Earth, under my control."

George was confused. This was impossible. No simple vampire should be able to break through his training, his own abilities, his protective spells.

Eric chuckled. "But I could not have done it without the resources of my former sect. Or without the power of the Hellmouth."

George looked in horror as the red orb grew.

"You are not entirely to blame," Eric continued. "I had you under a mastery spell. It was easy to do, after I killed your brother. You weren't paying attention to much, other than your own guilt and shame. To amuse myself, I taught a local vampire a much cruder version of it to use on the locals. But I have refined my own gift over a thousand years, so that you would do whatever I require and not even realize you are being controlled. Until now, of course. It is so much more satisfying to see one of the great and holy Druids realizing that he has damned the whole world."

"No!" George shouted. *How could this be?*

"You have control of your voice, but nothing else." Eric smiled. "Now complete the spell. Pick up the knife. Sacrifice the girl."

"No!" George said again, but he could feel his fingers curl around the hilt, feel his arm lift the knife above his head. Willow was tied to the makeshift altar before him.

"Take some consolation, George," Eric continued. "There is no way, now, to avoid the blood. The spell has gone too far. It demands blood, or it will destroy us all, and probably all of Sunnydale besides. Now, kill her and let's get on with it."

No! He would not be a party to this any more. He would find a way to reverse this spell. He struggled to bring the knife back down to his side, but only succeeded in keeping it from lifting any higher.

"What?" a young woman's voice called from just behind them. "You're throwing a party and we weren't invited?"

Without even turning around, he knew it was the Slayer.

Buffy ran into the room in front of the others, ready for action.

Willow was tied to a table in the middle of the room. She appeared to be out cold. The two others stood to either side of her, George dressed in ceremonial robes, Eric in basic vampire black.

"Kill her!" Eric demanded of George. "Kill her now! Once the spell is truly begun, I will bring things here from the Hellmouth that will swallow the Slayer whole."

George appeared to be struggling with the knife in his hands, like he was having second thoughts. Or maybe the knife was. Buffy decided she'd try to push Eric back first, then disarm the Druid.

"Oh, that sounds just yummy," she called to Eric. "But I don't think I can stick around. I do, though, hate to kick and run."

She whirled, aiming one of her patented Slayer kicks at his midsection.

But Eric was no longer there. Buffy almost lost her balance and had to come to a running stop.

"Watch out!" George called. "He's a Druid! He can fool you into thinking he's somewhere he's not!"

Eric was suddenly at George's side. "If you cannot kill the girl, then I will!" He reached for the knife.

Buffy kicked his hand away.

"Got you that time!" she called.

George screamed as he turned the knife on himself and cut a long, red gash on his arm.

But the red circle was growing, always growing, now the size of a manhole cover. And there were sounds coming from the other side—moans, and screams, and strange, strange laughter. But none of the voices sounded like they were having a good time.

"We have to stop it!" George called. "We have to stop it now!"

"No!" Giles said.

They had rushed quickly through the old building, led by Dave to that room where his uncle was conducting the spell. But the room was lit by flashes of a horrible light, and small fires burned in corners of the floor and on the walls.

They could not rush in there. In the next room, the Hellmouth was creeping into the world. If they drew too close, they might be consumed.

"It's not safe in there!"

"That much I guessed," Oz agreed. "But Willow's in there!"

"Buffy, too!" Ian added.

Giles squinted, attempting to see into the increasing glare. The two men inside appeared to be having an argument.

"Do you have any way to protect us?" he called to Dave.

"Only my uncle knows the spell!" the young Druid replied.

"Stay back!" Giles called to the others. There had to be some way to get in there and get back out again. If only he could wrack his brain and come up with something.

A new flare shot from the growing disc of light at the room's center. The entrance to the Hellmouth was growing stronger.

In a moment, they would have to try and rescue Buffy and Willow, no matter what.

George had been such a fool.

He had given this Eric everything he had wanted: a way to open the Hellmouth and even a young woman to be sacrificed. And now, through his stupidity, he was going to unleash upon the world the very thing he had tried so hard to prevent.

The gateway was growing larger. Already, he could see shadows on the other side, things eager to break into this world and destroy.

And Eric was correct. The spell was out of George's hands, and Eric was adding to the power by blood. If he could not sacrifice Willow, the vampire would force George to sacrifice himself, just to keep the passage open.

But blood was only one component of the spell. It might control the gate, or it might close it. George had spoken with the other elders, debated the ancient rites, until he knew every aspect that the Druids remembered. The spell needed blood. But with the proper incantation, the blood could end the spell as well.

George's mind was very clear. He could hear countless voices on the other side.

"Please, free me."

"I can bear it no longer."

"Give me souls and I will give you anything."

He thought he saw eyes within the fires—eyes and

mouths and hands—things that wished to take solid form if they could only step through the gate. They were very close. The spell would let them through.

Eric was laughing. "It is my time now! I will destroy you all!"

There was no helping it. George had brought this power to the edge of the world. He would have to force it back.

He still had the knife.

He raised it, and plunged it quickly into his own stomach, drawing the ancient blade all the way across. That should provide the blood.

But if he was not careful, his internal organs would spill out onto the floor. He clutched the wound together, and, saying those five words that would end the spell, leapt into the growing red orb.

He was surrounded by fire. By placing himself there, his burning form would close the way, cauterize the wound. He would be the seal that would keep the world safe from the Hellmouth.

He only had an instant to scream.

Everyone stopped when the circle disappeared.

"Buffy?" Willow opened her eyes and sat up.

"What happened?" Buffy said.

"My uncle sacrificed himself to end the spell," Ian explained. "For now, the magic has completely gone out of this place.

"The magic is gone?" Buffy turned to the figure in black. "Then Eric is only a vampire. I know how to deal with vampires." She pulled a stake from her bag.

Eric rushed at Buffy with a roar.

Buffy set herself to meet his change, certain she could avoid his fangs and stake him. She reached out to grasp his wrist.

But he wasn't there. He had avoided her counter attack. He was as fast as any vampire she'd ever fought.

"Slayer!" Eric whispered.

She almost looked at his face, before she remembered the mastery spell. It had killed Kendra, it could kill her as well. Perhaps the Druidic power was gone from the room, but who could say if the ancient vampire magic was gone as well?

She couldn't let Eric look her in the eyes.

"Look at me, Slayer!"

But Buffy was already on the move, watching his hands, his feet, anything but the eyes to tell her what he might do next.

"I don't know," she said lightly. "You've seen one vampire, you've pretty much seen them all."

Eric roared even louder than before. She watched his form approach, shifting her weight to one side, and noting how he shifted direction to counter her new position. He wanted to get her off balance, twist her around so he could reach her neck.

Two could play a game of surprise.

She took a step backward, dropping her stake hand low as if Eric's charge frightened her, and all she could think of was escape. Eric shifted again, rushing straight at her now, eager for the kill.

She fell back one more step, her feet now firmly planted to give her extra balance. She rose up to meet the charging vampire, grabbing one of his lunging arms. She pulled the arm forward, letting the vampire's own weight flip him into the air and over her head. He landed on his back.

An instant later, Buffy's stake was in his heart.

"Wow," Ian said.

Buffy gave an all-in-a-day's-work kind of shrug. "Hey, without the Druid stuff, he was nothing special at all."

Chapter 25

JOYCE WOKE UP.

Over the last few days she'd had the strangest dreams; dreams that all seemed to mean something.

This last one, though, really took the cake.

She'd meant to talk to Buffy about them, see if her daughter had any insight into the dream images. Not that her daughter would ever take the time to listen to her, especially lately. But after that last dream, it was probably just as well.

It was about one of Buffy's friends, one of the boys. Except, in the dream, he wasn't so much a boy as a—dog, maybe?

It could have even been a wolf.

Joyce could see the symbolism of this dream right away. A boy as a wolf? This was one mother's worry—and a pretty typical one, too—that her daughter didn't need to hear.

Oh, well. This last one had been a much quieter dream, without all the sinister shadow figures talking about the end of Sunnydale. Maybe it meant those earlier, upsetting dreams were over. Joyce would be just as glad if they were gone.

The earlier dreams had felt all too real, but this new one—a boy who was also an animal—

Who ever heard of such a thing?

It was almost morning.

They had all gathered back at the library one more time—all of the gang, and the three younger Druids, too.

"Well," Giles admitted, "it may not have worked out exactly as we planned, but we did succeed."

"Was there ever any doubt?" Buffy asked. At everyone's look, she went on. "All right, so there was a lot of doubt. But we always pull through in the end."

"That's our Buffy," Willow agreed.

"Ian and I have discussed this," Giles continued, "and we can see no ill side effects of the spells Willow and Cordelia were placed under."

"So I'm good as new?" Willow said.

"Maybe even better," Oz agreed.

"I'm glad that's over with, too," Cordelia added, "even if I did have to miss the Spring Formal." She smiled. "Of course, Xander's promised to make up for that."

"For the rest of my natural life, apparently," Xander agreed. "Formal dances when we're ninety."

"We can only hope," Cordelia added.

"Now, I've got a question," Buffy asked. "Why did you guys turn your backs on us when the Druids were first around?"

Xander grinned a bit sheepishly. "I thought I'd go off and help them, they'd teach me some moves—I could become, you know, like a Slayer's assistant."

Buffy shook her head. "Unfortunately, the only job opening I have is for Slayer's friend."

"That reminds me," Ian said. "I've got to apologize to Oz. Without our uncle here, I'm afraid we can't do much for your lycanthropy."

Oz shrugged. "Oh, well, If you're ever back in town . . ."

"Which reminds me," Buffy interjected, "now that you guys have helped us save the world, what are you going to do next? Take a little vacation in Sunnydale?"

Ian shook his head. "I wish that we could. But we have to go home and report to the elders. Eric's influence might go far beyond my Uncle George. And we may have to search for others of his kind."

"Oh," Buffy said in a very small voice.

"But before we go, Buffy," Ian continued, "I have to show you something."

"Oh?" she asked on a more hopeful note.

"Yes. I'm afraid I left it out in the hall." He walked across the room and took Buffy by the arm. His brothers turned to follow but he held up his hand. "Give us a minute here, people."

He guided her outside the library. Buffy didn't see anything out of the ordinary.

"What do you want to show me?" she asked.

"I'm afraid it's only me . . ." He put his hands gently on her shoulders. "If you don't mind?"

Mind? What was there to mind?

They kissed.

Ian smiled at her. "I would never have forgiven myself if I hadn't done that once."

"I won't forgive you if you don't do it again," Buffy replied, leaning into him.

"I'm sorry we have to leave so soon," Ian said when they were done. "Maybe I can get back here and see you some time."

Buffy smiled. "Hey. Maybe I can go to Druid summer school."

"Look," Ian pointed at the golden light filling the windows down the hall. "The sun's coming up. And it will keep coming up, thanks to what we did last night."

Buffy nodded her head. "Yeah. It almost makes up for the fact that, in about an hour and a half, I have to be back in school."

Ian nodded. "And my brothers and I really have to go."

They looked to each other, leaning in close enough to—

Cordelia burst from the library.

"Xander Harris! I don't know if I ever want to speak to you again!"

Xander came trailing after her. "So I suggested we

do a few things without a tux? What were you thinking about? Formal swimming?"

Ian waved to Buffy and went into the library to fetch his brothers.

Buffy sighed. But it was a good sigh.

It was the beginning of just another day in Sunnydale.

Return to normal.

About the Author

Craig Shaw Gardner has written twenty-odd novels and perhaps one or two that are not so odd, including the *Dragon Circle* series (*Dragon Sleeping, Dragon Waking,* and *Dragon Burning*), *A Malady of Magicks, A Bad Day for Ali Baba,* and *Revenge of the Fluffy Bunnies,* as well as the novelizations of such films as *The Lost Boys* and *Batman* (a *New York Times* bestseller).

Born and raised in Rochester, New York, Craig managed to escape and currently lives very close to Boston, Massachusetts.

THE WATCHER'S GUIDE

The official companion guide to the hit TV series, full of cast photos, interviews, trivia, and behind the scenes photos!

By Christopher Golden and Nancy Holder

Published by Pocket Books

1492-01

BUFFY THE VAMPIRE SLAYER™

As long as there have been vampires, there has been the Slayer. One girl in all the world, to find them where they gather and to stop the spread of their evil and the swell of their numbers

Child of the Hunt

By Christopher Golden and Nancy Holder

Return to Chaos

By Craig Shaw Gardner

The Watcher's Guide

(The Totally Pointy Guide for the Ultimate Fan!)

By Christopher Golden and Nancy Holder

Based on the hit TV series created by Joss Whedon

Published by Pocket Books

POCKET BOOKS

2022-01